Following MAGGIE

NEW YORK TIMES BESTSELLING AUTHOR

M MORELAND

Dear Reader,

Thank you for selecting Following Maggie to read. Be sure to sign up for my newsletter for up to date information on new releases, exclusive content and sales. You can find the form here: https://bit.ly/MMorelandNewsletter

Before you sign up, add <u>melanie@melaniemoreland.com</u> to your contacts to make sure the email comes right to your inbox! **Always fun - never spam!**

My books are available in paperback and audiobook! You can see all my books available and upcoming preorders at my website.

The Perfect Recipe For **LOVE**
xoxo,
Melanie

Following Maggie by Melanie Moreland
Insta-Spark #7
Copyright © 2022 Moreland Books Inc.
Copyright © 1190606
ISBN Ebook 978-1-988610-80-1
ISBN Print 978-1-990803-85-7
All rights reserved

MORELAND
BOOKS INC.

Edited by Lisa Hollett of Silently Correcting Your Grammar
Cover Design by Feed Your Dreams Designs
Cover Image Photography Adobe Stock SonyaChny

INSTA-SPARK COLLECTION

When you want a bit of naughty along with the nice.

Insta-Spark Collection from M Moreland are complete standalone reads with one thing in common - lots of sweetness and a guaranteed HEA. Instant attraction, little angst - love and happiness abounds in this collection.

\#GetYourKissOn \#ASprinkleofSugar
\#ASweeterRomance

CHAPTER ONE

MAGGIE

Airports were lonely places in the dark of the night, but especially so in the middle of a snowstorm. It was unnaturally quiet and empty with all the planes grounded, the skeleton staff talking quietly among themselves.

With a sigh, I shifted my backpack higher and moved away from the counter toward the window. Outside, the snow beat against the panes, the wind wild in its fury. I leaned my aching head on the cold glass, watching the storm swirl and rage outdoors.

Turning around, I scanned the terminal. People were scattered everywhere—those who were silly or hopeful enough not to listen to the reports of the sudden storm and plane cancellations were now stranded, or those, like me, who hadn't been able to get a hotel room. My plane should have flown around the storm and been fine, except for the unexpected problem with the engine, forcing an emergency landing just before the airport closed to all traffic. I had been in the back of the plane, and by the time I'd made it to the front of the line, the hotel rooms the airline was able to provide were long gone. I had accepted the travel voucher for another flight, a food voucher I could use in the terminal, and their apologies with a smile. The woman I was talking to managed to grab me a small pillow—smiling in gratitude when I told her I already had my own blanket in my pack. Listening to the people cursing and complaining at the airline staff, I was flummoxed. It wasn't as if they caused the storm preventing us from getting out of the city or the fact that because of the same storm, they couldn't even take us off the airport grounds.

I glanced at all the people, noticing most of the seats and spots against the walls were taken. The terminal was well lit, and numerous people were sleeping or using their phones and tablets. There were even long lines at the few payphones still in the airport as people tried to contact their loved ones. I felt the sudden rush of sadness. I had no one to call. No one was waiting for me to come home or cared where I was or that I would be late arriving at my destination. I pushed down my sadness and concentrated on what I would do until my flight was able to leave.

Investigating, I noticed an escalator leading down to some of the other, smaller gates. I paused, looking over my shoulder—I could go back through security into the larger main terminal. It probably wouldn't be as busy out there. I could find a spot to sit and watch the storm, but then I decided I would see enough snow over the next while, and what I really needed was some sleep. I headed down, wondering if perhaps it might be quieter below. At the bottom, I hesitated, then grinned in relief, because the area was almost deserted. The lights were dimmed, there was no staff at the gates, and only a few people were relaxing in chairs. I walked to the far corner, sitting down in one of the empty rows and pulling my backpack off my weary shoulders. Leaning forward, I stretched out my back with a small sigh of satisfaction. Sitting back, I closed my eyes, only to realize I should have taken a couple of Tylenol. With a groan, I got up and found a water fountain, swallowing the pills I had dug out from my pack. Seeing as I was right beside a washroom, I went in and washed my face and hands, brushed my teeth, and ran a comb through my hair. Feeling a bit fresher, I made my way back to my little corner, frowning when I saw I had company.

Across from my spot, a man was stretched out, already sleeping. His legs were bent at a funny angle, pulled tight to his body, and his head buried on his arm that was tucked under a scrunched-up jacket. On the floor beside him sat a bulging backpack resting against the seat and a battered guitar case. He was dressed in a white T-shirt and jeans, his feet clad in dusty work boots. The way he was curled up, his T-shirt had ridden up over his pants, exposing a wide expanse of his naked back. His jeans were pulled down, the waistband of his underwear peeking over the edge. Tilting my head, I read *Fruit of the Loom* written across the banding. Feeling like a stalker, I found my eyes drifting lower, settling on his ass.

His well-shaped, very firm-looking ass. The angle he was bent at showed it off to perfection. Squinting, I could even see two dimples resting just over the swell of his ass cheeks, and the sudden desire to reach across and touch them made me actually sit on my hands so I didn't do exactly that.

I frowned, wondering if I should move. Maybe he wanted privacy. Internally, I snorted—as if anyone could find privacy in an airport. Obviously, like me, he had sought out the quietest place he could find, because he wanted to sleep.

Which was a very good idea.

Shoving my backpack under my feet like a stool, I shut my eyes and leaned my head back. But I couldn't get comfortable. I shifted a little and tried again. I used the pillow I'd been given and attempted to curl into the seat, but the metal bars dug into my side and the thin cushion under me offered no relief at all. I turned the other way, trying to find a more comfortable position, throwing an envious glare toward the fine-assed, sleeping man. He seemed pretty cozy.

I watched as his shoulders moved in a continuous, slow rhythm, his breathing deep and even. I tried matching my breathing to his and felt myself relax and my eyes drift shut. A loud noise behind me startled me, and I sat back up to see a woman had dropped a large, overstuffed suitcase. I turned around and attempted once more to relax, but this time, it didn't work. I was never good at sleeping while sitting up. My slumbering neighbor made a low groan, his arm twitching a little before he resettled, and I frowned. He was lying down—stretched out across a few seats. Maybe I should try doing that. I stood and pulled on the wide, metal bar separating the seats, but it didn't budge. I pushed and pulled, but I couldn't get it to move. I moved to the next set of seats and tried again. Obviously, some of them had to pull up so you could lie down. Ass-man had figured it out. Surely I could, too.

However, I had no success. I sat down, frustrated. Looking across the aisle, I wondered if maybe only certain rows allowed you to move the handle out of the way. Cautiously, I tested a couple in his row, tugging hard on the handles, but none of them budged. Finally, in desperation, I circled around and warily leaned over the back of the seats he was sleeping on to see how the arm lifted. I was shocked when I realized the arm wasn't missing. Mr. Ass-man was curled right around the metal—so tightly it was digging into his stomach. I shook my head—it had to be uncomfortable, yet still, he slept. Unable to resist, I stared at his slumbering face. He was handsome. Beyond handsome. He had turned a bit, so his entire face was on display, his dark brown hair in wild waves around his temples. Thick, arched eyebrows slanted over his eyes. Long, dark, full lashes rested on high cheekbones. A sharp jaw was covered in thick scruff, the color slightly lighter than what was on his head. Full, pouty lips were partially open, his pink tongue resting on the bottom lip invitingly. I frowned at the dark circles under his eyes but understood better how he was able to sleep in such an awkward position. He was exhausted. Now that I could see him, I realized that, even asleep, he wasn't in total rest. His hand moved, fingers twitching constantly. His eyebrows flexed and contracted as his mouth frowned and pursed. Another low groan escaped his lips as a soft pleading "No," came out. His hand moved, lifting and seeking, his fingers flexing mid-air.

I felt the strangest need to comfort him. I wanted to run my fingers through his wild hair and soothe him, hold his hand and stroke the rough-looking skin so he would relax. When his hand moved again, I slipped mine into it, squeezing the wide palm lightly. Instantly, he seemed to calm, and his face relaxed. His hand flexed and held on to mine.

My gaze strayed over to my backpack. I wondered if I should cover him with my blanket and if there was any way of sliding the airplane pillow under his head, to make him a little more comfortable. I wanted to do something, help in some small way. Why, I had no idea, but the urge was overwhelming. I had to get my hand back first, though. I glanced back down, only to freeze in place.

His eyes were now open—staring right at me. Wide, startled eyes, so green it was like losing oneself in a deep forest. I felt my cheeks burst into flames at being caught leaning over him and staring.

I waited for the anger. The yelling that would start any second.

Instead, his full mouth curved into a slow, deep smile.

"Hello."

CHAPTER TWO

SEBASTIAN

I woke from my restless sleep, senses on alert. Dragging in a deep breath, I felt a strange sensation hit my chest at the sweet scent that filled my head. It was light and floral—like walking through a mass of lilac trees on a warm summer day, their scent rising up and enveloping me in their soft fragrance. I knew, even before I opened my eyes, someone was close to me.

I opened my lids slowly, staring transfixed at the girl who hovered over me, like a protective angel. My hand was wrapped around hers tightly. I blinked, unsure if I was dreaming or not—she looked so unreal in the dim light I wasn't certain if I was truly awake. Long russet-brown hair hung over the back of the seat she was leaning against. The thick strands tickled my wrist, and the desire to move my hand and wrap it around the tresses was strong.

She was looking past me, her blue eyes thoughtful. She was biting her bottom lip—her teeth worrying the plump skin, and I wanted to save the flesh from the torture she was inflicting on it. I felt no fear seeing her bending over me, or the fact that she was touching me. Instead, I felt only a curious warmth from her closeness. Her gaze shifted, her lovely eyes meeting mine, widening as she realized I was now awake. A deep red blush stained her cheeks, her teeth now sinking even deeper into that lip.

A rush of hot, fast desire tore through me as I gazed at her. I wanted to sit up and drag her to me. Cup her face and feel the heat of her skin under my fingers. Taste that tortured bottom lip. Bury my face into her neck and breathe her in as I wound my fingers in that glorious hair.

And then I wanted to kiss her.

Like I had never kissed anyone in my life.

The idea made me smile.

Her eyes were wide and fearful, and I knew I had to make the first move.

"Hello."

She blinked, looked at our entwined hands, and blinked again. Then she started to talk—very fast.

"You were asleep. I just wanted to see how the arm things went up, and I was checking. I wasn't staring—

I really wasn't staring. Okay—well, I was, a little. Because you're gorgeous. Like *wow* gorgeous. But I didn't know that when I was looking for the arm thing. You're gonna have bruises. You know that, right? In your stomach—from pressing into the metal thing. I was gonna move away, but then you looked sad and started muttering, so I thought you needed someone to hold your hand that kept moving." She finally drew in a deep breath. "I'm sorry."

I frowned, unsure what part of that paragraph she had just spat out I should respond to. So I started at the end. "You're sorry? For holding my hand?" I smirked at her. "Or staring? Or calling me 'wow gorgeous'?"

"Are you mad I'm holding your hand?"

With a start, I realized I was, indeed, still clutching her small hand within mine. "No."

"The staring part, then—you're mad about that?" She started gnawing on that bottom lip of hers again.

"I suppose I should be. You are invading my privacy and personal space after all."

"But you're not?" She sighed—a deep huff of air that lifted her hair so it brushed against my wrist once more.

"No." I had to laugh. She was rather cute. I squeezed her hand, brushing her knuckle with my thumb.

"Thank you for checking on me—even if you were trying to figure out the, ah, armrest."

"That's what it's called!" She grinned in triumph. "I always forget words when I'm tired."

Feeling strangely regretful, I released her hand. "You should get some sleep, then."

Groaning, I unfurled my legs and rolled off the seats, swinging my arms and stomping my feet. I ran my hand over my stomach, which was surprisingly tender. Maybe she was right and I would have bruises. I had been pushed into the metal bar fairly hard. I stopped trying to uncramp my muscles when I realized she was staring. "What?"

"Holy shit. You're tall." She looked across the seats where I'd been napping. "How'd you even fit?"

I sat down heavily and scrubbed my hand over my face. "I was so tired I didn't even notice."

"Did your flight get canceled?"

"Yes, but I've been here all day. My friend dropped me off earlier today—or yesterday, I suppose. My flight wasn't until later, but it was the only way to get here. After he left, I discovered I left my wallet at his place. It took me forever to get hold of him. I could still check in for my flight since I had my passport, but I had nothing else. By the time I got in touch with him, the airport was closing and the roads were too bad to get my wallet to me. He's going to try in the morning. If he can't make it, he'll mail it to me."

"Oh. That's awful."

I nodded. "The storm hit so fast—I guess no one expected it to move in this quickly." He chuckled. "So I've been stuck here most of the day."

"Wait, if you had no wallet, what did you eat?"

"I had five bucks in my pocket. I got a coffee and a bagel."

"When was that?"

I shrugged. "About noon, I guess."

She was out of her seat like a shot and hurried away, leaving me gaping after her retreating form.

What had I said?

She disappeared around the corner, and I shook my head. I didn't even know if she was coming back. Maybe my protective little angel was slightly crazy. I relaxed in my seat, grinning at the thought and running a hand through my messy hair. I needed a haircut. No doubt it would be the first criticism my father would have when he saw me.

I noticed a backpack and purse sitting on the floor across from me, as well as one of those airplane pillows. They must belong to her, which meant she had to be returning.

I grabbed the pillow and leaned my head back. I still had no idea where she'd taken off to.

I looked out the window at the empty runway. A storm was raging outside.

Where *could* she go?

Twenty minutes later, she was back, carrying a paper tray and a bag. I could hear her coming, her steps hurried, and she was panting as she rounded the corner. I opened my weary eyes as she approached, feeling myself smiling as I took her in. She wore leggings with a long shirt over them, topped with a jean jacket and a pretty scarf draped around her neck. Her hair was loose around her shoulders, and she gave off a bohemian vibe.

She was a slip of a girl—I doubted she would even come up to my chest if I stood in front of her. She would fit well under my arm when walking, her head resting below my shoulder. It would be the perfect height to nuzzle. I blinked at the strange thoughts.

She stopped in front of me, dropping to the floor. "I got you food."

"What?"

"You've been here all day. You're tired and hungry. I went and got you food."

"But you left your purse? I don't want you spending money on me." I frowned at her. "You don't even know me."

She waved her hand dismissively. "They gave me a food voucher, and the Tim's reopened a little while ago, so I got you some food." She stared at me with her expressive eyes. "They make great sandwiches. You have to eat."

"Are you always this bossy?"

"Pretty much. My dad…" Her voice trailed off, and a sad look crossed her face. "Yeah, I guess so."

The distressed look on her face made my chest hurt. I didn't know why, but I didn't like seeing her look that way. I lowered myself to the floor beside her and stuck out my hand. "I guess since we've already held hands, we're not strangers anymore…but I want to know the name of the little angel who's feeding me."

Her cheeks darkened, but she placed her hand in mine. "Maggie. Maggie Andrews."

I closed my fingers around her hand, enclosing it fully. It felt right, nestled into my palm, the warmth of her skin pleasant against mine. I lifted her hand to my mouth and kissed the soft skin. "I'm Sebastian Ruggers. It's a joy to meet you, Maggie Andrews."

Her eyes grew wide. "You kissed my hand."

"You held mine first."

She giggled. "Good point." Then she pulled her hand away and started unpacking the bag. She shoved two sandwiches and a container of soup toward me and set a coffee and milk beside it. "There're a couple doughnuts in the bag, too."

"What about you?"

"I got something." She pushed the pile again. "Eat."

I was about to protest but changed my mind since I was starving. If Chris was able to get me my wallet, I could return the favor if we were still stuck here. If not, I would mail her the money. Unwrapping a sandwich, I took a big bite, humming as I enjoyed the thick filling. Maggie ate her sandwich and sipped her coffee far slower than I did. We didn't talk much, but our eyes met often, holding briefly before one of us would look away—usually Maggie. I liked looking at her, seeing the color creep up on her cheeks, and how gentle her gaze was on me. Her eyes were bright pools of blue that gleamed even in the dim light.

I sat back, feeling full, then I stretched out my legs, sipping the coffee she had brought me.

"Thank you," I murmured with a satisfied sigh. "That was very kind of you."

"I try to be kind to people."

I had a feeling she didn't have to try too hard. Being kind was something I was sure came naturally to Maggie.

I smiled at her. "What do you do when you're not hanging out in airports, hovering over people and feeding them?"

Her smile fell, and she looked away. "I'm kinda between things."

I took another sip of my coffee. "I know that feeling."

"Where are you headed, Sebastian? Where's home?"

It was my turn to frown. "I don't think I'd call it home, but I'm heading to Vancouver."

"You don't look very happy about that."

I shut my eyes and drew in a deep breath. "I'm not."

Her voice was gentle. "Why are you going, then?"

I opened my eyes and looked into her soulful, patient gaze. I was about to tell her it didn't matter, but suddenly I wanted to tell her the truth—because, to me, it did matter. It mattered a lot.

"I'm a musician. At least, in my heart I am. I've been traveling, trying to get a break, get someone to listen to my music. Things had been looking up, and I thought I'd finally gotten what I needed. I spent all my savings recording a CD. I put everything I had into it—in fact, I borrowed money to finish it."

"What happened?"

"Nothing. A big fat nothing. The guy I worked with got a better offer and walked away. My so-called manager told me he was done and moved on. So, I'm left with a bunch of CDs I can't sell, no money in the bank, and not even enough to find a place to live."

"Oh, Sebastian, that's terrible."

"My friend Chris loaned me enough to get me here so I could try to start something back up. But it's not happening. So, now…" I sighed heavily. "I had to call my father, listen to his lecture and his lists of 'I told you so's' and accept his offer of a job."

"Well, maybe it won't be so bad. You can work and save some money for your music, then try again."

"Uh, no… My father's offer came with conditions, Maggie."

"What sorts of conditions?"

"No more music. No more chasing a 'stupid dream' that will never pan out. He told me it was time to grow up and act like a responsible adult, and the only way he would agree to help me was if I gave him the next five years. He paid off my debts, paid for this flight, and he'll find me a decent apartment to live in." I smiled sadly. "At least he didn't insist I live at his place. Not sure I'd survive constant criticism twenty-four seven."

Maggie gathered both my hands in hers, squeezing hard before releasing them. I found her touch oddly comforting. "You don't get along well with your father?"

"No. I've never been the son he wanted. My head and heart have always been too filled with nonsense—according to him."

"What kind of job will you be doing in Vancouver?"

"My father owns an insurance company." Just the thought made me shudder.

I regarded Maggie for a quiet moment, then the words starting to come faster. "Knowing I'll be spending my days behind a desk—pushing papers, attending meetings, issuing policies, dealing with claims, and be stuck doing it day after day, weeks on end—until the five years are up, makes me nauseous." I paused. "I hate insurance."

She nodded in sympathy.

I hung my head. "I know I should be grateful. Lots of other guys would be happy to have a job to go to. I just—"

"Just what?"

"I *know*, Maggie. I know that once I'm there, I'll never get out. I'll be there the rest of my life, growing old behind that desk, turning into a gray-haired old man like my father—angry and bitter at the world because life passed me by while I processed bits of other people's lives."

"You don't have anything else you can do?"

I shook my head. "No, I don't. I have a hundred bucks in my wallet that I forgot to bring with me. Not a cent left in the bank. I sold or pawned everything I had, except for my guitar." I glanced at the case reverently, then continued. "I spent the last three weeks pounding the pavement, looking for a job— anything that meant I didn't have to go back there. I tried to go back to construction, but I couldn't find anything permanent or even make enough to live on. I found nothing, and I can't keep living on Chris's couch. So I had to agree to my father's terms."

My head fell back against the seat. "I haven't slept much since then."

"Oh, Sebastian."

"Pretty pathetic, yeah? A twenty-five-year-old guy going home to Daddy. A real loser."

"You're not a loser!" she hissed vehemently. "Life has dealt you some bad breaks. There's nothing to be ashamed of in asking your dad for some help." She sniffed. "He sounds like a pompous ass, though."

I chuckled. "He is."

"What about your mom?"

"She died when I was a kid." I stroked the top of the guitar case. "This was hers. She loved to play, and she sang like an angel." I paused and swallowed. "I don't remember him being so disconnected or mean when she was alive, but once she died, he cut himself off from life…and me. We seemed to do nothing except butt heads after that—it's one of the reasons I left."

"I'm sorry."

I grabbed her hand again and shifted closer so our knees were touching. Somehow, I felt better when we were touching. We were still alone in this part of the airport, our own quiet little corner in the vastness of the building. "What about you, Maggie? Where's your home? Is that where you're headed?"

There was a long pause before she spoke.

"I don't know," she whispered. "I hope so."

CHAPTER THREE

I furrowed my brow at her words. They were filled with so much sadness, I could feel it. "Can you tell me?" I asked quietly.

Our gazes locked and held. Sitting this close, I could see the sorrow in her eyes, and I squeezed her hand, wanting to offer her the same comfort she had given me.

"My parents divorced when I was young."

I nodded for her to continue.

"I lived with my mom until I was a teenager. She got remarried—again—and I was tired of moving around and being in the way. So, when my dad offered to let me come live with him, I said yes. He lived in a small town outside of Calgary. It's very pretty there—lots of mountains."

"How did that work?"

She gave me a sad smile. "Dad was great. Quiet, but a good parent. He worked a lot—he was the principal of the local school and a volunteer firefighter, plus he was on the city council. I went to school and worked part time. We got along well, and I was very happy. My mom got divorced a couple years later, got married again, and then divorced—again." She shrugged self-consciously. "She was never one to stay put very long."

"A free spirit?"

"That's being kind, I think."

"Oh?"

"I was grateful to go live with my dad. My mom was always dragging me all over. She'd hear of some great area to live, with lots of opportunities for *her*, and we'd go. I lost count of how many schools I went to, how many places we lived. I can't remember most of the names of my mom's boyfriends or husbands who came and went. I never stayed anywhere long enough for me to get close to anyone, so I didn't have many friends growing up. I was too busy making sure the bills were being paid and there were groceries in the house. I learned early on if I didn't want to be hungry, I needed to fend for myself."

I frowned at her description. "That sounds rough, Maggie. Lonely."

She nodded. "It was. But with Dad, I found some stability. I made a couple of friends—one, in particular. I did well at school, and I liked looking after him." She sighed wistfully. "Maybe because he looked after me in return. I finally felt as if I had a home, you know? A place I belonged."

"What happened?"

"My mom continued to move to different places—I only saw her a few times. I started to go to university, and she called one day, out of the blue. She was… sick."

"I'm sorry."

She shook her head, her eyes looking everywhere but at me as a tear rolled down her cheek. "I gave up school and went to look after her. That was a year ago —she died two weeks ago today."

I clasped her hands tighter. "Angel…I'm so sorry."

She nodded as more tears coursed down her face.

"So, you're heading back to your dad now? Back home?"

She choked out a "sort of" and closed her eyes for a moment.

"Sort of?"

"Dad died a month ago," she whispered. "He had a massive heart attack and never woke up."

"Oh God…*Maggie.*"

Without another thought, I pulled her into my arms, holding her tight. Sobs racked her body, with hardly a sound coming from her. Only the softest little cries in relation to how hard she was shaking in my arms. I cursed myself—here I was complaining about my father who was removed but at least still here, and she had suffered the loss of both her parents within a few weeks.

"I couldn't leave Mom to go to Dad's funeral," she sobbed out. "She was so ill at that point, and there was no one else who could stay with her. I couldn't even tell her—she never knew. They held a memorial for my dad without me there."

I held her closer. She'd been suffering this all alone. Watching her mother die, knowing her father was already gone. I marveled at her strength. She had somehow made it through all that pain.

I let her cry. I didn't try to hush her or tell her placating words of how things would get better. I simply held her until she wasn't sobbing anymore. I had the feeling she'd been holding everything in so long, she needed to get it out.

Eventually, she pulled back, rubbing her face with her sleeve. "Sorry," she mumbled. "You didn't need to see that."

Slipping my fingers under her chin, I lifted her face up, forcing her to meet my eyes. Her gaze was sad and weary, and she looked almost lost.

"It's fine, Maggie."

"I got your shirt wet."

"It'll dry."

She dug in her bag for some tissues, wiping her eyes and blowing her nose. She pushed her hand through her hair and sniffed, another tear running down her cheek. I caught it with my thumb, wiping it away. "It's going to be okay."

She nodded, the action moving my thumb so it brushed her mouth. Her damp, smooth, plump lips pursed and pouted slightly at my touch. The air around us suddenly changed, became static with heat. My grip on her face tightened as I felt the warmth of her breath drifting over my thumb. I moved my hand, my forefinger now tracing her bottom lip. "So soft, my angel. Your lips are so soft."

Her eyes widened as I shifted nearer, slipping my hand around the back of her neck. I lowered my head a touch, thrilled when she lifted her chin, her face coming closer.

"Maggie—"

"Sebastian—"

"I'm going to kiss you now."

"Yes, please."

I pulled her to me, covering her mouth with mine. Warm, supple lips melded to my harder ones. She curled her fingers into the back of my hair, holding me close. With a small groan, I reached out, yanking her onto my lap and deepening the kiss. My tongue met hers, sliding and twisting in long, sweeping passes —stealing her breath and making it mine. The airport around us faded away. All that existed was this sweet girl in my embrace. I folded my arms over her back, creating a cage, holding her tight. She made the faintest little sounds, tiny whimpers and gasps that ignited my passion. She stroked the back of my neck restlessly, returning my ardor in full. I hardened when she rolled her hips, grinding into her and groaning.

The sound of high-pitched giggles startled me, and I drew back, gasping for air. An unamused-looking woman shook her head at me as she grabbed the toddler she was chasing into her arms.

"Public place, young man," she admonished.

Maggie's head was buried in my chest, her voice muffled. "It was private until you showed up."

I tried to hide the grin pulling at my lips, failing completely.

The woman's husband took the child from her arms and tugged on her. "Let them alone, Mary. I remember when we took every chance we had to lock lips." He winked at me as he escorted them away, and I couldn't resist winking back. I watched them go up the escalator, then returned my attention to the girl I was holding. I dropped a kiss onto her head, nuzzling the fragrant hair.

"They're gone."

She looked up, embarrassed, but the sadness from earlier gone. "I guess it's a good thing we were interrupted."

"I guess so." I hesitated and cleared my throat. "I don't, ah, usually go around kissing random women in airports."

"Where do you usually kiss them? The bus station?"

I laughed at her quick wit. "No, Miss Bossy. I don't usually kiss women anywhere."

She arched her eyebrow playfully. "You do it very well for not kissing us *anywhere*."

I lowered my head, brushing her lips. "Oh yeah? You liked that, did you?"

"Sebastian," she whispered.

"Maggie."

"Please."

I couldn't stop myself. I wanted to feel her mouth on mine again. I jerked her hard against me and crashed my lips to hers. Instantly, the world disappeared once more, and all that was left was us. Her mouth, her warmth, and the blistering heat I could feel building. Moments passed as I kissed her, devouring the taste of her, somehow knowing I would never get enough.

The voice on the loudspeaker startled us both, and we pulled apart, shocked to see the lights were now on at full brightness. We listened to the drone of the bored voice informing us the runways were still shut down and no planes would be departing until further notice. I glanced at my watch, surprised to find it was almost six in the morning. Meeting Maggie's eyes, I smiled at her while caressing her back. "Guess we're stuck for another little while."

She nodded and moved off my lap. Immediately, I missed her being close, and I caught her hand. "Where are you going?"

She stood and stretched. "I'll be right back."

She headed toward the restroom, and I leaned my head back, groaning.

What the hell was I doing? Making out with a total stranger in a deserted airport. Telling her my life story. Sharing things with her I'd never told another person.

I had to be crazy. At some point today, she'd get on her plane and I'd get on mine, and we'd never see each other again. We both had lives we had to find and live—both in different provinces and with different circumstances.

Yet, as I watched her come back, my first instinct was to hold out my hand, smiling as she took it. I pulled her down beside me. "You should get some rest."

"You, too."

I stood. "We both will. I'll be back."

I studied my reflection in the mirror of the men's room, then splashed some water on my face. I had already sent my father a text so he knew I was stuck here indefinitely, and Chris still couldn't get here with my wallet because of the storm. I knew all that should bother me more. Normally, I would be impatient, cursing the weather and pacing the airport restlessly, but instead, I grinned at the pretty girl waiting for me by the wall.

Lowering myself down, I arched an eyebrow in her direction. "We gonna sleep on the floor?"

"It has to be more comfortable than stretched out across those chairs."

I rubbed my sore stomach reflectively. "You're probably right."

I took the little pillow she had in her hands and placed it on my lap, patting it in invitation. She looked at me, her brow furrowed. "Are you sure? I was going to sit up and you lie down."

"Nope. I slept earlier. Your turn. C'mon."

She curled up, her head on my lap, staring up at me. I ran my hands through her thick hair, stroking her forehead the way I remembered my mom doing when I was a kid. I loved how Maggie leaned into my touch, pressing her head to my hand. "Relax, angel," I murmured. "My turn to watch over you."

Her eyes fluttered and drifted closed, her shoulders curling inward as her body grew heavy. I didn't stop stroking her head, even when I knew she was asleep. Something about her made me want to make sure she was safe and cared for. That she knew she was both—however brief our time was together. My hand stilled as I realized how sad the thought of leaving her in a few hours made me.

I shook my head at the strange thoughts and leaned back into the wall. I must be overtired and overthinking everything.

This was just a fleeting moment in my life—in both of our lives.

A layover.

Nothing more.

CHAPTER FOUR

SEBASTIAN

I woke up, confused. Blinking, I opened my eyes, and I realized I was staring at a wall. I shifted a little, my muscles protesting as I moved. I was stiff, sore, and unsure how I ended up lying down. The last thing I remembered was sitting on the floor next to Maggie and her falling asleep curled beside me.

Maggie.

My body jerked, then relaxed as I understood why I was so warm. Maggie was still snuggled into me, except now we were both lying on the floor, her back against the wall and me in front of her like a human shield. She was pressed up against me, my shirt held tight in her fist, her face buried in my chest. Our legs were entwined, and the little blanket she had earlier was draped over top of us. My head was resting on my folded arm, the nerves tingling as circulation began to flow again. I had my other arm draped over her, holding her close. An announcement on the loudspeaker, calling my name, made me ease my arm out from under Maggie and sit up. At the same time, my phone buzzed, and I grabbed it out of my pocket.

"Yeah?" I rasped.

"Sebastian, man, where are you?"

"Chris?"

"Who else?"

"Where are you?"

"I'm at the airport. I've been paging you."

"Shit. I fell asleep. How did you get here?"

He chuckled. "I borrowed my neighbor's snowmobile. Wicked. I'm by the check-in counter."

"I'll be right up."

I glanced over to see Maggie watching me, still lying on the floor.

"Chris is here with my wallet."

She sat up, nodding. "You should go get it. You should also see if they have any information about flights."

I stood, stretching, trying to get the kinks out of my neck. "I will. I'll have to come back through security, so I might be a bit. Give me your ticket—I can at least ask for you at the same time. I'll bring coffee too, okay?"

She smiled up at me, all sleep-rumpled and tired-looking.

I thought she was the prettiest girl I'd ever seen. I bent down and kissed her forehead. "Don't run away, Maggie Andrews."

Her eyes crinkled. "Where else am I gonna go, Sebastian?"

It took all of my control not to tell her wherever it was, I would go with her. Instead, I grinned back. "I'll be back."

"I'll be here."

Even knowing that, I hated leaving her.

Part of me felt guilty for not wanting to hang with Chris. After all, he had driven all this way with my wallet. I was glad when he told me the snowmobile was outside and he couldn't stay anyway. He did reiterate his invitation to stay with him longer, assuring me he'd help me find a job. I smiled in gratitude as I shook his hand. I had to face my father and accept my life. Chasing after a dream that would never happen needed to end.

I watched him leave, then made my way through the line at the ticket counter, only to find out I wouldn't be getting out of here for a few more hours. The snow had finally stopped, they were clearing the runways, but the airlines had a huge backlog of people to move. I inquired for Maggie's destination and was told the same thing. I found out we would actually be on the same flight until we got to Calgary. There, she'd get off the plane, and I would continue on. Knowing I had more time with her somehow made the wait seem less tedious. I was still smiling as I slid down the wall beside her a short time later. Our bags were piled beside her, and she was resting against them, only opening her eyes as I nudged her with my foot.

She accepted the coffee and the news, neither of us upset for the further delay.

I grinned as I showed her my boarding pass. "We're on the same flight."

"How?"

I shrugged. "Charm, mostly."

She giggled. "No, really. How?"

I laughed with her. "She offered me a direct flight earlier, or this one." I hesitated but continued, "I chose this one."

She seemed genuinely surprised. "Why?"

Wrapping my hand around hers, I squeezed her palm. "So I could have a little more time with you."

She smiled at me, leaning forward. I closed the distance and brushed my lips to hers. "Is that okay?" I asked.

"Yeah," she whispered. "So okay." She winked. "Stalker."

I bumped her shoulder. "Only for you. You have to go and get your pass. She's holding the seat beside mine for you."

"Charmed her for that, too?"

"My charm works on mortal women, Maggie. It's just you airport angels that it fails on."

She stood, brushed off her pants, then grabbed her ID and ticket. She looked at me, a small frown on her face. "Your charm more than works, Sebastian. Trust me."

Then she turned and hurried away.

Even though I knew she'd be back, I hated watching her leave.

She brought back bagels and more coffee—obviously, she was as addicted to the stuff as me. All around us, the airport was coming to life—the tarmacs were being plowed and salted, more people started arriving for flights, and the counters were bustling. Planes were preparing to take off soon. We still had a few hours before we would depart, and I was content to sit with my little angel, people-watching and talking.

We talked about anything and everything. I was amazed how much we had in common. We both liked the same types of music and books. We liked the company of others yet enjoyed being alone. Maggie filled her hours reading, while I wrote music. She even convinced me to play a song for her on my guitar. Watching her expression as I strummed quietly and sang to her caused my heart to clench. Her eyes were misty when I finished, and she leaned close, this time kissing me, her lips soft against mine. "You have a gift," she whispered. "You can't give it up. Find a way of holding on to it, Sebastian."

Her quiet, sincere words made me smile. They also made me want to say things I couldn't. I felt overwhelmed by her and by the emotions she stirred within me. Knowing our time was drawing to a close made me edgy.

Time seemed to be going by far too quick.

"Tell me about the place that made you feel like home."

She sighed. "It's a tiny town about two hours outside Calgary called Riverstoke. One of those small places where everyone knows everyone, you know? People walk more than they drive. You can smell the forest, see the stars, and hear the birds in the morning."

"Sounds great."

"I love it there."

"And your house?"

"It's average size. Three bedrooms, a nice-sized living room, a big eat-in kitchen, and a small bathroom. Dad tried to keep it up, but it needs updating and a lot of work. He wasn't a good handyman."

"Will you stay there?"

"For a while. I have to decide what to do. See if I can find a job, if I can afford to fix it up and stay, or sell it."

Her voice sounded sad, and I frowned at her. "What do you want to do?"

"I want to stay. Settle down and make a life. I've always liked it there. It's a small town, but lovely, and the people are friendly. If I can stay, I will. It always felt like home, you know?"

"If Chris and I were there, we'd help you."

"Is that what Chris does?"

"Yeah—he's very good. He works for a home-building company. If they'd been hiring, I could have tried to stay. I'm pretty handy."

"It must be hard on your hands, though?"

"At times—but at least I could have done both. Now, the only time I'll be playing my guitar is when I'm alone. Part of my father's conditions. No music."

"That's so wrong."

"I had no choice. I had to agree."

She looked at her hands, her fingers moving restlessly. "There's a bar in Riverstoke—they're always looking to hire people. My friend Amber and her husband own it. And they do open mic nights." At my startled look, she quickly added, "If you ever wanted to visit, I mean. Bring your guitar."

"You'd like that?"

"Yes."

"I'd like that too…" My voice trailed off at the thought of spending more time with her after we left here.

"But?"

I turned so I was facing her. "I like you, Maggie. I like you a lot."

"I like you too."

"You're going to a new life, and I have to somehow come to terms with what sort of life I have waiting for me. I don't want to start something with you that's only going to end up with heartache for both of us." I reached for her hand, holding it tight. "I don't know when I could come and see you, or even if I could for a while. In the meantime, I don't want you passing up other opportunities."

"Other opportunities?"

"Maggie—you're lovely. Truly beautiful. You're the whole package. Some guy, probably several, will see you and want to take you out." I had to pause and swallow at the pain just thinking about the next words caused me. "And once they get to know you, they'll want you to belong to them. I can't even bear the thought of that."

"So you think it's best to not even try?"

"I can't ask you to put your life on hold while I try to figure out mine. That's not fair—to either of us."

She yanked her hand away, looking annoyed. "What if I said I wanted to? Maybe I'm not interested in *other* opportunities."

I sighed. "You should be. I'm not a good horse to hedge your bet on."

"I disagree."

"I adore you for thinking that. But this is simply a moment in time. For both of us."

Hurt filled her eyes. "I thought it was more—I thought you felt it too."

"I do, but it can't happen. I refuse to let you think it can. I won't lie to you."

For a moment, she was silent. Then she nodded and turned away. "Thanks for being honest."

I swallowed the painful lump in my throat. I was being anything but. I wanted to tell her we'd call and text. I would come and see her whenever I could. I wanted to explore this—whatever this was—with her. I'd never felt anything remotely close for another person as I did for her, even in the short time since we'd met. She'd shown me more care than anyone had in my life in years, and I wanted more. However, I was too worried if I said all that, I would hurt her— more than I just had. Dragging it out would only be worse, I told myself.

"I'll change my seat if you want. I understand if you don't want to be around me anymore."

She shook her head. "No, Sebastian, it's fine. We're, ah, good."

I reached over and cupped her chin, turning her face to mine. Her eyes were sad and yet still so gentle as they looked at me. I stroked my thumb over her soft skin. "I wish, more than you know, it could be different."

"So do I." She smiled and lifted her shoulder, trying to lighten the moment. "I could have used your construction expertise to help me fix up the house."

Before I could say anything, she drew back. "I'm kinda tired. I'm going to try to sleep. You'll keep watch on the bags?"

"Of course."

She turned away and slouched down, her head on her backpack. It took everything in me not to reach over and turn her toward me so she cuddled against me with her head on my lap. I knew I had lost the right to ask her now.

I glanced at my watch. Our flight was due to leave in two hours. If it was on time, that meant I had only a few more hours with Maggie.

Six more hours of pretending that what I had just told her was the truth. Of ignoring how it felt when I kissed her. How right her hand felt in mine. Of how the thought of saying goodbye to her was making my chest ache. How my head hurt at the mere thought of her walking away from me.

These were going to be the longest and most painful hours of my life.

CHAPTER FIVE

SEBASTIAN

We both tried to be what we'd been before I lied to her. But it didn't work. When she sat up, after having pretended to sleep for a while, we were awkward and the conversation stilted. I asked her more questions about her little house, offering suggestions when she described the creaking porch and the roof that always leaked in the one corner. In her own way, she was as quietly supportive as before, encouraging me to find a way to continue with my music and find a life that fulfilled me.

"I don't think you can be happy without your music, Sebastian. It's part of you. For your father to take that away is simply wrong."

She was right about that; I was angry with my father for that nonnegotiable condition. Music meant so much to me, and I resented him for making me leave it behind.

But if I were given the choice, I *would* give it up—if I could keep her.

But I had no choice.

I couldn't have either of them.

We boarded the plane, and I let her slip into the window seat. Outside, the sun was bright on the whiteness of the snow, the airport now busy and filled with activity.

I noticed her fidgeting, and I leaned closer. "Does flying make you nervous?"

She nodded and allowed me to hold her shaking hands. She didn't even object when I lifted them up and kissed her knuckles. She calmed down once we were airborne. All around us, passengers were sleeping—the entire plane quiet. So many had been trapped all night, and now that they were on their way to their destinations, relief won out and they relaxed, knowing the end of the long wait was in sight.

Maggie leaned her head back, closing her eyes. I noticed the dark circles under them, as well as the dampness that lingered in the corners, and cursed myself because I knew I had a hand in both. She was trying so hard to pretend she was fine, but I knew she wasn't.

I wasn't either.

I kept her hand in mine and watched her, my mind going as fast as the plane we were in. The more the miles flew by, the more the ache in my chest grew. Maggie would walk away from me soon, and I'd never see her again. I'd head to BC and the life my father insisted I had to live, and she would make her own way in the small town, hundreds of miles away from me.

I would go to an apartment I'd never seen and live there. My father would make sure it was decent and I had what I needed to live. Maggie would go to her little house and try to fix it up and make a life for herself. She would struggle to make ends meet and fight to hold on to the place she thought of as home. My father's plan would enable me to live well, but it wouldn't feel like home. Like *my* life.

Both of us would struggle for different reasons.

Both of us surrounded by people, yet alone.

I'd always felt alone—except for the past few hours. With Maggie beside me, I hadn't felt that way. For the first time in my life since my mother died, I felt as though I was complete again—as if I mattered.

I mattered to Maggie.

She mattered to me.

If we were together, things would be different. If I *chose* differently, both our lives could change.

Thoughts, ideas, and images began taking shape in my head.

If I changed my mind.

If I asked Maggie to let me go with her. Not to visit, but to stay.

We could find and build a life we both were happy in —together. Fixing up her little house and making it ours. I could find a job; I could do anything. I wasn't afraid of hard work. She said the bar in her little town hired a lot. It would be a job that would still allow me to play my music without my father's restrictions. I could do it all—work and make music and be happy. It was never the limelight that I sought, simply the chance to play and share my music.

I looked at Maggie, studying her face. She'd encourage me to do both. I knew she would. We could figure out a way for her to go back to school and finish her degree. It wouldn't be easy—any of it, but we could do it.

I suddenly saw two very different paths.

A life in which I did as my father asked and planned for me. A stable life of security and blandness. One without music or light, where I was comfortable but simply existed.

Or…

I could start one of total unknowns. Living in a strange city, with a woman I barely knew, yet wanted to know so much more. A life where we would have to struggle to make it work, but I knew would be filled with laughter and love and where music and happiness would be paramount. A life where the smile of the small, russet-haired angel next to me would be the best reward I could ask for.

I sucked in a deep breath.

I was about to do something drastic.

Even more drastic than asking my father for help.

I was about to ask for another chance and change my future. Risk it all to find a home where I belonged. I was about to follow Maggie home.

<hr>

MAGGIE

I heard his fast intake of air and felt Sebastian shift in his seat, his hand holding mine tighter. It took everything in me to remain still and pretend I was sleeping. I wanted to talk to him and tell him he was wrong. To beg him to see he could come to Riverstoke with me and find a life there. We could figure it out together. Neither of us had to face the future alone—without the other. He didn't have to give up his music, and I didn't have to continue my lonely life. But he'd been honest with me and told me it, *us*, wouldn't happen, so all I could do was get through this flight and then say goodbye.

I would hate it, but I would do it.

His body pressed into mine, his warm breath drifting over my skin. "Maggie," he whispered. "Open your eyes for me, my angel. I know you're not asleep."

I did as he asked, surprised to see how close he was. His face was inches from mine, his warm green eyes staring at me. My heart raced faster with his closeness.

"What?" I whispered back, hoping he wasn't going to apologize for not wanting me the same way I wanted him again.

"How did it feel?"

I frowned at him. "How did what feel?"

"When I kissed you. How did it feel?"

I stared at him, unsure how to answer. "I don't know if I can answer that."

"Can I try to help you figure that out?"

"Yes."

He buried his hand into my hair, drawing my face to his. His mouth covered mine, and he kissed me—in a way I'd never been kissed before. Long, deep, sensuous passes of his tongue. Playful nips of his teeth as he pulled my bottom lip between his. Low-pitched groans that let me know how he felt. He possessed me totally. Tenderness, passion, want, desire, and longing were in that kiss. Deeper and deeper we sank into the emotion he stirred up between us. I held him tight, my fingers digging into his skin, never wanting to let him go. He held my face snug to his with one hand, while he had me locked against him with his other arm. It was only the clearing of someone's throat that pulled us apart, and even then, he refused to let me go. He pressed his forehead to mine.

"Do you know what it felt like to me?"

I shook my head, my heartbeat thundering in my ears.

"Like I was home. Like it was the start of forever."

I gasped.

Why was he saying this?

"Did it feel like that to you?"

"Yes," I breathed out.

He buried his head into my shoulder. "I can't let you go. Even though I should, I can't."

"I don't want you to."

He raised his head, his gaze intense. "I want to go with you."

"Then come."

"I don't have anything to offer you. I'm broke, and once he finds out I'm not showing up, my father will disown me."

"All I need is you. You're more than enough. The rest, we'll figure out together."

"I've never been enough before—for anyone."

"You are. You are to me."

He leaned forward, clutching my hands. "I don't know what this is between us, Maggie. All I know is that I don't want it to be over." He stared at me pleadingly. "I don't want you to leave me. I don't want to go and sell insurance."

"What do you want to do?"

"I want to go with you. Help you fix up your little house. Make it ours. Get to know you better. Find a job packing groceries or pouring drinks in the bar. I don't care. As long as I get to come home and see you there, it won't matter."

"Sebastian…"

"We can make a life together, Maggie. You want roots, I want to belong to someone. We can be there for each other." He paused and searched my eyes. "Each other's home."

I nodded eagerly. I wanted that. I wanted him.

"Are we crazy?"

He grinned. "Yes."

"I'm good with that."

He kissed me again—soft, gentle kisses of adoration. "I found an angel in the airport."

"I think I found you."

"Yeah, you did."

My eyes filled with tears.

"Are those good tears?" he questioned quietly. "Or are those 'God, why did I ever go near that weirdo in the airport' tears?"

"Good tears."

He smiled widely. "Yeah?"

I nodded, beaming at him. "I want you to come home with me. We'll figure it all out together, Sebastian. Each step. Neither of us has to be alone anymore."

He lifted my hand and kissed it. "I'm going to love you hard, Maggie Andrews—I already know that. I'll love you until you don't remember what your life was like before I showed up. Are you prepared for that?"

"I can't wait. I'm going to love you back just as much."

He pressed his lips to mine once again.

"Then let's go start our future."

I smiled at him.

"Our future."

CHAPTER SIX

SEBASTIAN

The cab pulled up in front of a small house, silent and still in the early morning darkness. Wearily, I stepped out, offering my hand to Maggie to help her from the back seat. I grabbed our bags from the trunk, while Maggie paid the driver with the twenty-dollar bill I had pressed into her hand, silently arching my eyebrow at her to protest. She accepted the bill without argument—too tired, I figured, to fight about something so trivial.

After getting off the plane, we took a bus into the city, then sat in the terminal for hours, waiting for yet another bus that would take us to the place where her house was located. When we finally pulled into the small town of Riverstoke, we were both exhausted. Maggie wasn't even sure there would be a cab around at four a.m., but luckily, there was. We'd both been quiet the past few hours, lost in the thoughts inside our heads. I wondered if she was regretting her impulsive offer of having me come with her. I wondered briefly if I had made the right decision. But when her hand slipped into mine and she settled her head against my shoulder on the bus, the sense of calm I felt made me realize my decision was the right one. I only hoped she felt the same.

Standing on the sidewalk, I smiled down at her. "I hope you have a key."

She held up the dull bronze key with a nod and a smirk. "I hope there's heat and electricity."

I picked up the bags, while she walked ahead of me.

"We'll figure it out."

The porch stairs creaked, and I noticed a few of the rails were broken. I began to create a "to-do" list in my mind. I saw the lean on the one side of the porch she had spoken about, and I knew that was one of the first things I would have to look after. I was already certain it was causing the small leak she had described.

Inside, she flicked the light switch, sighing in relief when light flooded the hallway. "I had texted Dad's neighbor and told her I was coming back soon, but I hadn't given her a date. I wasn't sure if things would be working."

I moved forward, shucking off my coat. The air was cool, but not cold. While Maggie went ahead and turned on a couple more lights, I moved through the kitchen and down the hall to the thermostat and turned it up, pleased when I heard the furnace immediately kick in. Returning to the kitchen, I looked around. The house was modest but nice. The eat-in kitchen was large, plus a decent-sized living room with a fireplace. I knew upstairs were two large bedrooms and a smaller one that Maggie had thought we could use as an office. I poked my head in the doorway off the kitchen and checked out the laundry room. It was surprisingly spacious, and I quickly added to my list. A second bathroom would work well there.

Maggie opened the refrigerator and let out a pleased sigh. "I think Eleanor must have brought a few things over."

"Is that your neighbor?"

She nodded. "I haven't met her yet. She moved in just after I left. Dad spoke highly of her and her husband. They were incredibly kind to him." She paused a moment. "They've been so sweet and helpful to me with their emails and looking after the house until I could come back."

I crossed the room and pulled her into my arms. "We'll figure out a way of saying thanks." I nuzzled her head. "But right now, we need some sleep, then we can make some plans."

"You have to call your father."

I sighed. "I know." I wasn't looking forward to that. At the moment, he thought I was still stuck in the airport.

She looked up at me. "You should do it now while I go see what condition the rooms upstairs are in and find some towels. I need a shower."

"That sounds good."

She hesitated. "I know it's not going to be a pleasant phone call, Sebastian."

I snorted. "That's an understatement. He's going to be furious."

"You need to make sure this is what you really want, before you call," she murmured, her worry etched on her face. "I understand—"

Shaking my head to stop her thoughts, I stroked her cheek with my finger. "It is. But is it what you want? Are *you* sure, Maggie?" I looked around the room. "I can see us here together already—laughing at the table, eating dinner, watching movies, and cuddling on the sofa." I slipped my hand over hers, squeezing it. "If you're sure, so am I."

"I am sure. I want this. I want you with me."

Brushing my lips across hers, I smiled. "Then go have your shower, and I'll make my call."

"It's not too early?"

I shook my head. "My father believes in 'early to bed, early to rise.' He's up at four a.m. every day."

She shuddered a little. "I'm not much of a morning person."

I grinned and kissed her cheek. "Neither am I. See how right we are for each other?"

That made her smile. Bending down, she grabbed her bag. "I'll be upstairs when you're ready."

"Okay."

I sat down, staring at the phone, knowing how bad this was going to go. Before I could take the coward's way out, I dialed his number and hit send. He picked up on the first ring—his usual terse greeting.

"Sebastian."

"Hello, Father."

"Are you still stuck in the airport? I expected to hear from you late last night."

"No, I'm in Alberta. That's why I'm calling."

"I find it hard to believe they're still backlogged and bumped you off there."

I swallowed hard. "They didn't bump me off. I bumped myself off."

There was silence for a moment. When he spoke again, it was with his carefully controlled tone—the one I hated the most. "Why would you do that, Sebastian?"

I stood and began to pace the room as I spoke. "I'm not coming to BC."

I heard the sound of a fist hitting something—no doubt the wall or whatever piece of furniture he was the closest to.

"Get your ass on the next plane, Sebastian. I'm serious."

"No."

"What did you just say?" he uttered slowly.

"I said no. There's no point in me coming there—I won't stay. I don't want to sell insurance. I don't want to give up music. I'm just saving us both a lot of disappointment."

"So, what is your plan, then? Begging on the street? Playing that stupid guitar and asking for quarters?" he snapped. "You irresponsible ass! Have you not figured it out yet? You don't have the talent, or the money, to keep doing this. Stop your damn daydreaming and grow up!"

I tamped down the hurt caused by his words. He'd always hated music. I thought it reminded him too much of my mother. So did I. In a way, I supposed that was why he wasn't overly fond of me either. I took in a few deep breaths before speaking again.

"I know you're angry, Father, and I'm sorry. But I'm not coming. I'm staying here."

"Where is here, exactly?" he demanded.

I didn't want him to know where I was. For some reason, I wanted to keep it to myself.

"I'm not far from Calgary."

"What the fuck are you doing there?"

"I'm staying with a friend. I have a lead on a job, and I'm going to try it here."

"If you don't get your ass on a plane today, Sebastian, and this fails—and we both know it will—I won't help you. This is your last chance. The offer ends today. I'm tired of your immaturity."

"Why can't you let me live my own life? Why can't you support me?" I cleared my throat of the emotion that was building. "Why do you dislike me so much? Because I look like Mom? Act like her instead of you?"

"Don't you talk about your mother."

"Of course not. I can't talk about her or how you ignored me since she died or how I feel. The only things we can talk about are your expectations and how I disappoint you at every turn!" I shouted, my anger getting the better of me. "I'm never enough, and it's not going to change—ever!"

"Oh yes, throw in the neglected child and the dead mother card. How badly you were treated and the cruel life you've led."

I sat down, too tired to stand anymore. "I don't want to do this anymore. I'm not coming. I'm staying here where I have a chance of being enough for someone and I can make a life I enjoy living."

"What are you talking about?"

"I met someone. She believes in me, and I want to see what happens between us."

"Oh, for *fuck's* sake. Now you've, what, fallen in love? In a day?" he snarled. "Did some whore cozy up to you, all sweet and loving, pretending to care? Promising you a happy future?"

"Don't," I hissed into the phone. "Don't you dare say a word about her, or about us. You know nothing. You don't know me, and you certainly don't know her."

"Grow up!" he yelled. "Either you get back here right the fuck now, or I'm done with you!"

I shook my head, even as a tear slid down my face. He would never change, and I had to end this, for my own well-being. "Take care of yourself, Father."

After I hung up, I sat on the sofa, not moving for a while. Finally, I stood and, with heavy treads, went upstairs, not surprised to find Maggie sitting on the top step, looking sad.

"Hi," I murmured. "You heard, no doubt."

"I'm so sorry, Sebastian."

I shrugged and sighed heavily. "I expected it…but I guess I still hoped."

"What can I do?"

I smiled at her. She had obviously had a shower—her hair was wet and hanging down her back, and she was in a set of warm pajamas with thick socks on her feet. Beneath the socks, her toes wiggled. She looked adorable—and exhausted.

I touched the moving toes. "What's going on here?" I teased, wanting to make her smile.

"I do that when I'm nervous."

I bent and kissed her forehead. "Don't be nervous with me, Maggie. I'll shower and maybe sleep for a bit, if that's okay?"

"This is your home now, Sebastian." She gave me a soft, reassuring smile. "You don't need my permission."

Her words made my heart race. Her gentle acceptance made me relax.

She held out her hand, and I took it, following where she led me. The bathroom was still steamy from her shower, and she handed me a towel. Then her nervousness showed again, and she began talking fast.

"I put a pair of sweatpants and a shirt on the counter. I gave them to my dad for Christmas—he obviously never wore then since the tags are still on. They'll be a little big on you, but at least they're clean and warm. And you don't have to be naked. Unless you like to be naked, but I thought you might want to wait for that. At least until you find out that I snore. Because there is nothing less sexy than snoring." She paused and turned her head to look down the hallway. "I made up the bed in my room for us. It's a queen, but if you prefer, I can make up the guest room bed too, if you want to sleep alone. 'Cause, again—the snoring thing. Not really snoring but grumbling. I talk and mumble, and my dad used to say I growled. And I have cold feet." When I looked at her, trying not to laugh at her word vomit, she kept talking. "Anyway, I figured we'd sort of already slept together in the airport...well, not *slept*, slept together, but whichever you want…"

I held up my hand, smiling a little more now. "I'd like to sleep with you, Maggie. *Sleep*, sleep, I mean. I liked how you felt all curled into me. I'll risk the grumbling and the cold feet." I ran my finger down her very warm cheek. "We'll move on to the other 'sleeping together' part when we're ready. No rush, my angel."

"Okay." She pointed to the door at the end of the hall. "That's my…um…our room. I'll be there, waiting."

Our room.

I liked the sound of that.

"Okay. See you there."

CHAPTER SEVEN

SEBASTIAN

I was warm and comfortable when I woke up.

Too warm.

Maggie was curled up tight to my chest, her arm wrapped around my waist, holding me close. I was no better, both my arms draped around her back, my hands buried in her hair.

It should have felt strange. All this *intimacy* should feel strange. But it didn't.

After my shower, I walked to the end of the hall where Maggie waited. She was already in bed, and it felt completely natural to lift the blanket and slide in beside her. Reaching over, I flicked off the light, and she nestled beside me. I drew her closer, wanting her warmth.

She had closed the curtains, the dim light shut out, so the room was dark. It wasn't where I had expected to be today, but it felt good—it felt right.

Emotion hit me as I thought about all that transpired to get me here, and tears burned, hot and heavy on my cheeks. A sob escaped my throat, and Maggie moved up, cradling my head on her chest, soothing me with her touch and quiet voice.

"It's okay, Sebastian. I've got you—let it out."

"He's not worth it," I mumbled, yet unable to stop the damn waterworks.

"He's your father, Sebastian. Whether or not he's worth it, of course this would upset you. Just let it out. When you wake up, we'll start fresh."

She held me until I fell asleep.

I couldn't remember ever sleeping so peacefully. It had only been a few hours, but I felt refreshed. I looked down at Maggie—*this girl*, this perfectly wonderful girl I barely knew—yet I trusted her more than any other person in my life. She offered me a level of faith I wasn't used to, one I wanted to measure up to. I wanted to give myself to her the way she offered herself to me—freely and without reservations. I wanted her to know me, and I wanted to discover everything that made Maggie Andrews so special. I never wanted her to regret opening her heart to me and asking me to stay with her.

Carefully, I slipped out of bed and made my way down the hall to the bathroom. When I was done, I spent a few minutes looking around upstairs. Her dad's room was actually a little smaller than Maggie's, and I grinned, knowing he must have given her the larger room. The third room was about the same size as his but had a great view of the forest behind the house. It would be a perfect place to sit and play music, looking at that view. I went downstairs and rummaged around the cupboards, finding the coffee, the cream in the refrigerator, then spent a few minutes figuring out the coffee machine, finally getting a pot brewing.

In the light of the day, I gazed around the rooms I had seen only hours ago, now taking in the details. I could see lots of small projects and a few bigger ones that I would need to do. I liked the fact that Maggie needed work done—it would make me feel useful and productive. I wanted to feel needed by Maggie. I had a feeling I was going to need her just as much.

When the coffee was done, I shoved my feet into my sneakers, grabbed my coat, and went outside. The sun was shining and warm on my face, although the air was cold and snow was everywhere. I sipped the hot beverage, enjoying the quiet of the area, until a surprised voice startled me.

"Hello?"

I turned and met the curious gaze of a woman walking up the driveway. She was holding a casserole in her hand but seemed puzzled as she stopped at the bottom of the steps.

"Hello." I smiled at her. "You must be Eleanor."

She looked even more surprised.

"I am. And you would be?"

I held out my hand. "Sebastian."

She shook my hand, still frowning. "I was expecting someone else."

I nodded. "Maggie. I know. She's still asleep. With all the delays, it was a long trip home for her, and she's pretty tired." I stepped back, indicating the door. "Can I interest you in a cup of coffee?"

She hesitated, and I had to laugh. "I assure you, Maggie is upstairs, asleep. If you want, I'll wait out here, and you can go in and check on her."

She shrugged sheepishly. "Sorry."

"Don't be. I'm sure you weren't expecting Maggie to drag home a stray."

"Is that what you are, Sebastian? A stray?"

The door opened behind me, and Maggie spoke. "No, he's not a stray. He was lost, but he's home now."

Turning, I pulled Maggie close, dropping a kiss on her head. "Yeah, I think I am."

Eleanor beamed at both of us, then reached over to hug Maggie, telling her how glad she was to meet her. Maggie started thanking her for all her help and looking after the house, so I stepped inside to give them some privacy, knowing her dad would be brought up and Maggie would get emotional. I grabbed some more mugs and poured the coffee, refilling mine.

When they came in a few moments later, I could see I was right. Maggie's eyes were misty, and I lifted her hand, kissing the palm before pressing it to my face in silent understanding. I took the casserole Eleanor had brought and put it in the refrigerator, then joined them to finish my coffee.

Eleanor was warmth personified. She listened to Maggie's story of meeting me in the airport, her eyes wide when she realized we'd only known each other such a short time. Then she shook her head. "You seem so right together."

"We are," Maggie and I stated in unison, then laughed.

"You don't seem shocked," I observed.

Eleanor grinned. "I met my Patrick on a Wednesday, and we moved in together that weekend. We were married a month later—that was fifteen years ago. Sometimes your soul just knows."

Maggie spoke up. "Your husband—he's a doctor, correct?"

"Yes. He's working today, but he's off tomorrow night. Maybe you and Sebastian would like to come for dinner? I'd love to get to know the two of you more. We're going to be neighbors after all."

"We'd love to, Eleanor. Thank you." Maggie beamed. I could tell how much she liked Eleanor already, and I had to admit it was an easy thing to do. I liked her as well.

"What do you do, Sebastian?"

I shrugged. "Whatever I have to. I'm going to take a walk later and put in some applications. I want to find a job and then start working on some repairs in the house for Maggie."

"You're a handyman?"

"I have a lot of construction experience. I need to see what tools Maggie has and what I'll need to get."

"Sebastian's a brilliant musician too," Maggie stated, sounding proud.

I lowered my head, feeling embarrassed. "I hold my own."

Eleanor clapped her hands. "You can borrow some of Patrick's tools. Why he has them, I have no idea. He's a brilliant doctor, but he can't hammer a nail to save his life. I have a list of things to be done, and I've been looking for someone to take on the job—if you're interested."

"I'd be happy to have a look. Are you sure Patrick won't mind?"

She chuckled. "The last time he tried to do a repair, I had to drive him to the hospital for stitches. The nurses had a good laugh when Dr. Ruggers became the patient. I doubt he wants to experience that again—his ego took a big hit that day."

I frowned at her. "Dr. *Ruggers*?"

"Yes?"

"That's my surname as well."

"Really? It's an uncommon name. Maybe you're related."

"My father never mentioned any family aside from the two of us, but maybe so."

"You'll have to chat with Patrick about that tomorrow." She stood. "Now, I have to go and do some errands. Do you need a lift anywhere, Sebastian?"

"No, I'll walk around, but thank you."

"Okay. Dinner tomorrow at six. If you need anything before then, just come across the street or call. Maggie has the information."

With a final hug to both of us, she left.

Maggie smiled at me shyly, and I drew her into my arms, grazing her cheek with my lips. "Hi."

"Hi."

"Sleep well?"

"I slept very well." She grinned up at me. "You're a cuddler."

I chuckled. "I think we both are. We were pretty entwined when I woke up." I dropped another kiss on her cheek. "I liked it."

"Me too."

"What are your plans for the day?"

"I have to go to the bank and the lawyer."

"Okay. I'll walk with you and investigate the job possibilities, and maybe we can meet somewhere after?"

"You don't have to have a job by the end of the day, Sebastian. Don't put that sort of pressure on yourself."

"I'm not. Honest. But I want to check it out, then make a plan." I pulled her a little closer. "This is a new start for us, Maggie. I'm excited. I want to move forward and begin my life with you."

"Okay, then."

I kissed her one more time.

"Okay."

CHAPTER EIGHT

SEBASTIAN

Maggie and I separated on the corner by the bank. She pointed out the bar she had mentioned, and we agreed to meet in two hours. It felt so natural to pull her close and kiss her before walking away. I turned around to see her watching me leave, her fingers on her lips. I grinned at her and winked, grinning even wider when she blushed and hurried away. I liked her reactions, and I hoped she never stopped showing me how my touch made her feel.

I wandered around, found the hardware store, the local diner, and a few other places, amazed at how friendly people were to me. I was greeted with a smile everywhere I went, and when they discovered I had moved here and would be around, they were quick to introduce themselves. By the time I made it to the bar,

I felt like a politician with the number of hands I had shaken. I was careful not to share exactly where I was living. I wanted to protect Maggie's privacy since I had no idea how well she knew any of them. I also wasn't sure how much she wanted people to know at this point, and I'd take my cue from her. When they asked, I waved my hand in the general direction and said I'd moved to the east end of town. Luckily, no one pressed me.

Maggie knew the owners of the bar and had specifically told me I could use her name there, so I entered the Keynote Bar and Grill, noting the two signs in the window. One read *Help Wanted*, and the other advertised *Open Mic Nights*. I was interested in both of them.

Stepping inside, I glanced around. The bar was quiet, but a few people were at tables and sitting along the polished wooden bar, sipping drinks. There was a small dance floor, and in the corner, a stage was set up. It was casual, bright, and clean. It also smelled delicious, reminding me all I had eaten this morning was some toast. I rather hoped Maggie would be early and we could eat together. The casserole Eleanor had left us, we could eat another time. We could have an early dinner here.

I approached the bar, sliding onto a stool. I could feel a lot of curious glances my way, and the bartender looked up from polishing glasses and offered me a nod. "Hey."

I smiled at him. He was tall, with wavy dark hair and a friendly face. His brown eyes gleamed behind the heavy frames of his glasses.

"Hello. Would you be Finn, by chance?"

He pushed off the back counter, setting down the glass he was working on. "Depends on who is asking, I suppose."

I had to chuckle. "I'm not serving any summonses." I held out my hand. "I'm a friend of Maggie's. Sebastian. Sebastian Ruggers."

He leaned forward, an easy smile on his face, shaking my hand. "Maggie, eh? Well, if you're a friend of hers, then welcome. Finn O'Connor." He shook my hand firmly, then he frowned. "I assume she's home?"

"Yes. We arrived back late last night. Or, early this morning, more like it. She's running a couple errands, but she'll be here soon."

He arched his eyebrow. "*We?*"

"Yeah."

"I imagine there's a story there."

"There is. Maggie will be here shortly, and I'll let her share it."

"I look forward to hearing it. I'm glad she's back, though. My wife's been worried about her. She'll be happy to see her."

I remembered Maggie had mentioned his wife, Amber, and said she was a whirlwind and kept Finn in line. The two women were good friends. Maggie's imitation of Amber made me laugh, and I was looking forward to meeting her.

"Can I get you anything while you wait?"

"A beer would be great."

"On tap?"

"Sure."

He slid a tall glass in front of me, and I took an appreciative sip.

"Anything else?"

I pointed to the window. "Actually, I'm interested in your signs."

"Which one?"

"Both," I stated honestly.

"You have experience?"

"I've done a few bartending gigs. I have my Smart Serve papers. I've done a lot of open mic nights too, in case you were interested." Smart Serve papers were required of anyone who served alcohol in Canada, and you had to have them completed before you could be hired.

He picked up another glass and started polishing it thoughtfully. "I hired someone for days already, so the only thing I have left is the Thursday to Saturday late shift. Four o'clock to closing, all three days."

He held up the glass to the light, inspecting it, then set it back in place and picked up another one. "Long hours, the pay isn't great, but the tips are usually pretty good. You get dinner with that as well." He winked at me. "My Amber runs the kitchen, as well as everything else around here, so I promise you the meal is good."

My mind raced. It wasn't ideal, but it was a job. It meant money coming in, so I could contribute to the house I'd be sharing with Maggie. Maybe on the days I wasn't working, I could pick up some odd jobs. Eleanor made it sound as if decent handymen were hard to find around here. "Okay, I'd certainly be interested. Do you have an application I can fill out?"

Before Finn could answer, a tall woman with auburn hair in a long braid came barreling out of the kitchen, her hands full. She served the table in the corner, called over to Finn for refills, stopped and chatted at another table, hugged someone leaving, then leaned against the bar, frowning at me.

"I don't know you."

There was no doubt; I was looking at the infamous Amber.

Finn spoke up. "This here is Sebastian. A *friend* of Maggie's. He's applying for the night job."

She hopped up on the stool beside me, her voice eager. "Maggie? Is she home?"

"Yes, she is. We just got back last night. She'll be here soon, I think."

"We?" She pursed her lips. "How *good* a friend are you, Sebastian?"

I chuckled. She was direct, this one.

"I'll let Maggie fill you in. I'm sure she can explain it better than I can."

"Oh, a story. I like the sound of this."

"Ask him his last name, Amber." Finn smirked.

She arched an eyebrow at me silently.

"Ruggers."

"Are you related to Patrick?" She clapped her hands. "I love Patrick!"

"I don't know. I met his wife this morning, and she wondered the same thing."

"I love this! Two stories!"

I grinned at her enthusiasm, not wanting to burst her bubble. The chances of finding family were slim. My father was an only child, so I doubted it—unless they were very distant relatives.

I glanced at Finn. "Can I fill out that application?"

Finn and Amber shared a look. It felt as if they were having a silent conversation, and unsure what else to do, I took another sip of beer. Finn nodded slightly and reached out his hand.

"You start Thursday."

I grabbed his hand, shaking it hard. "Really?"

"Yep. Amber will get you the paperwork to fill out and some bar shirts to wear. I'll show you everything on Thursday. I'm sure you'll catch on quick."

"I will. The open mic thing…"

"Why don't we see how you do bartending, and then we'll move on to that. Deal?"

"Deal."

I was bent over the bar, filling out the various pieces of paperwork—a pile of T-shirts and one long-sleeved shirt, all emblazoned with the bar's logo, beside me—

when the door opened and Amber blew past me. "Maggie!"

I turned on my stool, smiling as I watched Maggie being hugged by Amber. Our eyes met and held, our own conversation happening.

I missed you.

I was glad when Amber released Maggie and she came over. I tucked her to my side and felt her warm mouth on mine again as I kissed her thoroughly. I drew back, cupping her cheek. "Hey. How'd things go?"

"Good. Unexpected. I'll tell you later," she murmured.

"Everything okay?"

She nodded. "Just a lot to take in." Then she looked at the shirts. "It looks like you've been busy."

"I start Thursday."

She flung her arms around my neck. "That's great!"

"It's nights."

"We'll figure it out. What about open mic?"

"That's still up for discussion."

She turned to Finn. "He's amazing. His voice is…I can't even describe it."

"Maggie," I chided gently.

Finn chuckled. "It's fine, man. Your girl is proud. I'm cool with that." He winked at Maggie. "He'll get his chance, Maggie. Promise. I need the help more than I need someone on that stage right now. We'll figure it out."

"He better, Finn. Or you'll answer to me."

We both snickered at that empty threat. Finn towered over her by a foot and outweighed her by a good eighty pounds. I wrapped my arm around her waist, pulling her to my side and kissing her forehead. "Easy, Angel."

But her faith in me made my chest ache with her sweetness. No one had shown me that kind of faith since my mom had died. And the way Finn referred to her as my girl—I liked that as well.

I stood. "Come on. I'm starving. I'll buy us an early dinner, and we can celebrate, yeah?"

Amber appeared beside me. "Dinner is on the house, and it'll be ready in ten minutes. Meanwhile, I think Maggie owes me a story. Finish your paperwork, Sebastian." She linked arms with Maggie and dragged her away. I looked at them, shaking my head, then glanced back at Finn.

He grinned and shrugged. "Get used to it, man. Don't fight it, because it does no good. Just enjoy the ride."

I picked up the pen. Somehow, getting used to all this seemed…*right*. Easy—as if it was meant to be.

And so far, I was enjoying it.

CHAPTER NINE

SEBASTIAN

I stared at Maggie over my glass. She'd been telling me about her appointments and what had happened. "Your dad did what?"

"The house is paid for and is being transferred into my name. There was a small life insurance policy. It's not huge, but it's enough I can fix a few things up." She sighed. "I guess he worked really hard to pay off the house."

I wrapped my hand around hers. "He wanted to make sure you were taken care of if he wasn't around." I squeezed her fingers. "He sounds like a great man."

Her eyes misted over. "He was. I wish I had seen him one last time. Been able to tell him to his face how much I loved him."

"He knew, Maggie. I'm sure of it. You told me you talked to him a lot."

She wiped under her eyes and nodded. "I did." She straightened her shoulders. "And I told him every time we spoke."

I smiled at her affectionately. "Good."

"Mr. Jones told me the town is looking for someone to run the library."

"What about going back to school?"

She sat back, sipping her soda. "I think-I think I want to put that off for a while."

"Why?"

She was quiet for a moment.

I studied her. "I could help you fix up the house, you can sell it, and we can move closer to where you want to go to school, if that was what you wanted, Maggie. I don't want you to give up your dream because I've become part of your life."

She looked around and shook her head. "No, that's not the reason. I want to stay here. When we arrived last night, it felt as if I was coming home finally. I missed this town and the people in it that I knew. It just felt…right."

I drew in a deep breath. "Okay. But if you change your mind, I'd follow you anywhere you wanted."

She smiled at me. "Sometimes your dreams can change, Sebastian. Evolve. I want to stay here with you and make a life. I can do courses online if I want."

I winked at her. "So, I've become your dream, then?"

"I suppose."

"I might be a bit more of a nightmare at times."

She grinned. "I guess we'll see."

"I guess so." I leaned forward, my voice low. "I understand, though. I have to tell you—walking around, being greeted by strangers, all the smiles and hellos—it was nice. I felt comfortable. It seemed oddly right. Like I belonged."

"Yes!" She nodded eagerly. "You found a job. I'll apply at the library. We have the house. It's a great start. And we have each other."

I nodded. "That's the best part."

She smiled sweetly. "It's more than we had a couple of days ago."

She was right.

"So we stay and build a life."

"Together," she hummed, looking happy.

"Together," I repeated.

I liked the sound of that.

When we got back to the house, I wandered around, making a list of things that had to be done. I marked the items as I went in priority—the sagging porch and leaking ceiling were at the top of the list. They would have to wait until spring, though, since the ground was frozen, but I could at least go up on the roof and patch it for now. I was hoping that when we went for supper I could check out what tools Patrick and Eleanor had that I could borrow, so I wouldn't have to buy so many. I'd give her a deal on the work she needed done, so I could do things around here for Maggie.

For us.

I glanced toward the kitchen, where Maggie was checking out the contents of the cupboards. A week ago, I thought I'd be in my father's office, selling insurance and already hating life. I had no idea I'd be standing in a small living room, planning a new life with a pretty girl I found fascinating. I watched as she stood up on her toes, trying to reach something and not quite able to touch it. Twice, she tried to lift herself to the counter and failed. Her coordination was horrendous, and I was pretty sure it was a good thing she didn't make it. Setting down my list, I hurried to the kitchen and stood behind her, easily reaching over her head, grabbing the box she'd been attempting to reach, and handing it to her. She smiled up at me in thanks, and I dropped a kiss to her forehead.

"Stay off the counters, Maggie. I don't think climbing them is a good idea." I lifted the edge, showing her how broken they were. I didn't want her falling.

She chuckled. "I did it all the time when I was younger. Although I admit, they are worse for wear now." She traced a long crack with her finger. "I always wanted to fix up the kitchen. I love to cook."

She sounded wistful. Then her eyes widened, and she started rambling. "Not that I don't appreciate the fact that my dad left me the house. Or that he did the best he could. Obviously, paying off the house was more important than new kitchen cupboards. I sound ungrateful, don't I?" She worried her lip. "I don't mean to." She rushed on. "But I can see it in my head. How pretty it would be, how functional. How nice it would be if the floors didn't squeak." She shook her head. "I need to stop."

I pulled her into my arms and kissed her just to shut her up. She was amusing with her word vomit. I looked around the room. It was a good layout but had certainly seen better days. The cupboards sagged, the handles were mismatched, and the hinges rusted in places.

"It's not ungrateful, Maggie. Your dad would probably love the fact that you want to stay here and fix it up. We can plan it. Keep our eyes open for sales and people getting rid of appliances."

"Yeah?"

I nodded. "You never know what you're going to find. We can be patient. I can install a counter and floor—if we watch for bargains and do the work ourselves, it's doable."

Her eyes shone with excitement. "Really?"

"Yep, and I was thinking how easily we could add a small bathroom to the laundry room over there. We could do it all at the same time. Maybe I can convince Chris to fly out and help when we're ready."

She threw her arms around my neck, hugging me close. Chuckling, I lifted her to the counter, still holding her. It was easier than bending down—she was so tiny, my back ached from bending too long. She felt so right in my arms, though.

She tilted her face up, and I stared down at her, thinking of how it had felt when I opened my eyes at the airport and saw her. My little guardian angel, already taking care of me.

The air around us changed, warming. Her eyes widened, growing soft and filling with desire.

"Maggie," I murmured, pressing closer.

She sighed, sliding her hands up my neck, pulling my face down. "Sebastian."

Our lips met—softly at first. Brushing, touching, stroking. Her tongue slid along my bottom lip, and with a low groan, I yanked her tight, winding my hand in her thick hair and tilting her head, now ravenous for her. I was demanding, tasting and exploring her. She wrapped her legs around my waist, the quietest of whimpers deep in her throat as we kissed unendingly. I slipped my hand under her shirt, running my fingers up her spine, feeling the delicate bones and soft skin of her back. She fisted my hair, tugging gently.

With a low growl, I leaned closer, flexing my hips, my cock pressing into her. She tightened her legs, drawing me closer. In a heartbeat, I had her off the counter, striding toward the stairs, our lips never separating.

The phone rang, startling us both. I paused on the stairs, looking down at her. Her kiss-swollen lips beckoned me, but I could see the ringing of the phone had broken the moment. With a smile, I turned back, depositing her on her feet by the phone.

"To be continued," I murmured.

The next evening, we crossed the road to have dinner with Eleanor and Patrick. Maggie had made a cake, slapping my hands aside when I tried to steal icing from the bowl. Finally, she gave me the beaters to lick, pushing me away. I leaned against the counter, enjoying the sweet treat and teasing her as I told her the icing would taste much better if I could lick it off her skin. I loved the way she blushed at my words, although I decided it was something I wanted to try—and soon.

Eleanor greeted us with smiles and hugs, explaining Patrick had been called in on an emergency but would be home soon. She handed Maggie a glass of wine and told her to sit and relax. "I can show you all the things I want done while we wait!"

Laughing, I agreed and followed her around. Most of the jobs were simple—things I could repair or install easily. In the garage, I checked out the impressive array of tools they owned—some still in boxes. She told me with a laugh Patrick had bought many of them. "It makes him feel manly—even though he has no idea how to use them." Then she smirked. "He tries, the poor dear."

When I asked her about borrowing some, she was quick to agree. "Anytime, Sebastian. I'll give you the code to the garage, and you can borrow them anytime." She flashed me a smile. "As long as you fix all my stuff, too."

"You just hired a handyman, Eleanor."

"Great."

"Make me a list, and I'll start next week."

She clapped her hands. "Now I can order those cupboards I wanted for in here!"

I looked at the vast array of white cupboards already lining the walls in the large garage. "What's wrong with these?"

She wrinkled her nose. "I want stainless steel and wood—dark, thick wood."

"What are you doing with these?"

She shrugged. "I was going to throw them out. I don't want them. Any ideas?"

I stepped closer, inspecting them. They were simple, white, and still in good condition. They would be easy to match, and with new handles and a coat of paint, look like new. I could add new trim and molding, and they would be perfect. "If I pull them out without charge, can I have them?"

"For Maggie?"

I nodded. "She said how much she'd love to update the kitchen." I grinned. "Our budget could handle these."

She held out her hand. "You have a deal."

"Can we keep this a secret? I want to surprise her."

She smiled warmly at me. "Sebastian, we're going to get along just fine."

I laughed and followed her back into the house, already feeling at home in this new life I was creating.

CHAPTER TEN

SEBASTIAN

We had sat down to dinner, and were enjoying some wine, when Patrick arrived. He rushed in the side door, calling his apologies, kissing Eleanor, shaking my hand, and hugging Maggie, telling her how pleased he was to finally meet her. He attacked his dinner with gusto, sipping wine and telling tales from the hospital. He was of average height, his hair mostly silver, but his blue eyes were bright and intelligent. Kind. He was entertaining, charming, and effervescent.

He was also obviously in love with his wife, and the feelings were returned tenfold. The shared glances, the way he leaned over to stroke her cheek or touch her hand—they left no doubt as to their feelings. I could see Maggie and me, years down the road, being the same way. I was already very attached to her, and it had only been a few days. I was certain she was my future. As I picked up my wineglass, I caught her eye, smiling and sending her a wink. My smile grew wider as pink flooded her cheeks and she bit her lip.

Eleanor and Patrick both chuckled, and it was my turn to feel the heat in my cheeks. Patrick pushed his plate away with a contented sigh. "Eleanor, my love, that was delicious."

"Agreed." I nodded.

She smiled graciously. "Maggie brought dessert. Your favorite, Patrick, carrot cake." She stood, and Maggie jumped to her feet.

"I'll help, Eleanor."

"Thank you, Maggie."

They gathered the dishes and left the table, chatting amicably.

Patrick smiled at me. "So, Sebastian, Eleanor told me how you and Maggie met."

I stiffened, waiting for his lecture. I was prepared for a long, drawn-out diatribe about how foolish I was to give up a sure job and a safe life for a new life with a girl I barely knew, no job, and no guaranteed future. What he did say surprised me.

"Insurance, eh? What a horrid thought. I can barely stand buying it, never mind selling it." He reached over and clapped me on the shoulder. "And the added bonus of a girl who adores you? Who wouldn't jump at the chance of a new start? And this is a great place to do so. I love this town."

"My father didn't think so."

He studied me for a moment. "I understand your last name is Ruggers. And Eleanor tells me you come from Vancouver."

"Yes."

"My last name is Ruggers too."

"I've heard."

"May I ask your father's name?"

"Michael Anthony Ruggers."

He took a long sip of his wine. "And your grandfather's name—your father's father—was it Anthony Paul Ruggers?"

I frowned.

How did he know that?

"Yes. How—"

He cut me off. "And you—you are Sebastian Paul Ruggers?"

Now I was downright anxious.

"How did you know that? How do you know my full name? Or the name of my grandfather?"

Patrick didn't say anything for a moment. Then he leaned back and laughed. Big guffaws of mirth echoed off the walls. I stared at him, wondering what could be so funny about my father's or grandfather's names. Eleanor and Maggie came in, carrying cake and coffee, and sat down, looking at me. I shrugged, having no idea what was going on.

Eleanor shook her head. "Patrick," she admonished him. "It's not that funny."

"But it is," he insisted.

Eleanor glared at him, and with a final guffaw, he stopped.

He wiped his eyes, added cream to his coffee, and took a bite of cake, chewing it slowly.

"Great cake, Maggie."

She glanced at me, puzzled. "Um, thanks, Patrick."

He sat back and looked at me. "Sorry, Sebastian. I know you're confused. It's just…the situation. The irony. Karma is indeed a bitch at times."

"You're right, Patrick, I am confused. What situation?"

"What do you know of your family?"

"There isn't much to know. My parents were only children. My grandparents are deceased. My mother passed when I was younger. I have no siblings or any other family. That I know of, anyway."

He shook his head. "You do have family, Sebastian." He leaned forward, earnest, his elbows on the table. "You have me."

I gaped at him.

"I'm your uncle—well, half uncle, I suppose."

"*What did you just say?*"

"Let me explain."

"I wish you would," I huffed. "I don't know how you can be my uncle when my parents were only children."

"Your mother was, but your father had a half brother, Sebastian. Me. Your grandfather was my father."

"I don't understand."

"My full name is Patrick Anthony Ruggers."

"But you're…"

"Too young? Your father is fifty-eight, and I'm forty-two. I assure you, it's true."

"Why didn't I know this?"

"Why are you in Riverstoke?" he countered.

"Because I couldn't live the life my father insisted I lead."

"Your father didn't approve of me either—I was the result of his father's second marriage. He didn't approve of his father's new, younger wife, or me. He made that apparent my whole life, and when I was old enough to understand, he made sure I knew I wasn't welcome in his life." Patrick chuckled. "Not only was I a tainted blip on his perfect family, I was rather, ah, wild. I liked to live life to the fullest in my younger days. He made sure I knew I would never amount to anything and I was certainly not fit to carry the Ruggers name."

"I knew my grandmother died young, but I didn't know my grandfather had remarried. My father never mentioned that."

"That doesn't surprise me. He pretended we didn't exist and, no doubt, chose to leave out a lot of family history that didn't suit his superior attitude. When your father found out my mother was pregnant, apparently the news was not well received. He refused to have anything but the barest involvement with my parents after they married. In fact, he made their life so miserable, my father let him go to a private school, and he stayed in residence. Once I was born, he stopped visiting at all. He went to university in BC, and contact was sporadic at best. After my father died, we moved to Alberta. I saw your father a couple times when I was older, but he refused to even try to have a relationship." Patrick rubbed his chin thoughtfully. "He was very…"

"…inflexible," I finished for him. "Once he makes up his mind, there is no swaying him. He won't forgive me for coming here and not giving in to his demands."

"I'm sorry he did that to you," Patrick offered kindly, then grinned. "But can you see the humor? He didn't want me anywhere near him or his family. And now his son, my nephew, is living across the street and having dinner with me." He shook his head. "What are the odds?"

I sat back, completely blown away. My father had lied to me all my life. I thought he was all the family I had. "Did you ever meet my mom?"

"Yes. Once. She was a lovely woman, Sebastian. You remind me of her a great deal."

"Your dad died before I was born. I never met him."

Patrick looked sad for a moment. "He was older, but he was a good dad. He loved books and learning. He adored my mother and she him. They had a good marriage. It always bothered her that your father wouldn't even try to get to know her. She tried, but he refused all her efforts."

"Is she, ah…?"

He nodded. "She's alive. She's in a fifty-five–plus place in Calgary. She is going to be amazed to hear this, and I know she'll want to meet you." He paused. "If you want that, of course."

I sucked in a deep breath. "I would, Patrick. I'd like to get to know you, too. My father always refused to talk about his father much. He spoke of my grandmother on occasion, and I assumed he had the same sort of relationship with his father that I had with him. I always thought I had no other family."

Patrick smiled. "Well, you do. Eleanor and I are your family. My mother is a step-grandmother to you, and I assure you, once you know her, you'll love her."

Eleanor chuckled. "Connie is a hoot. She and I are great friends. When she finds out she has someone new to spoil, she'll go crazy. And wait until she meets your girl."

I looked over at Maggie, who had been silent this whole time. Reaching for her hand, I held it tight, not sure what to say. She smiled at me, squeezing my fingers, and I knew she understood. We'd talk this all out when we went home.

"Are you in contact with your father at all?" Patrick asked.

"He told me not to bother," I stated, remembering the sting I had felt when he uttered those words. "But I think he might be interested in finding out who my new neighbor is." I sniggered. "It would certainly get a reaction."

Patrick began to chuckle. "I wonder if he would even recognize me. I take after my mother except for my height and the early silver hair thing. She always said I had my dad's smile and brain, though," he mused, taking a sip of his coffee and a bite of cake. He chewed slowly, then swallowed.

"Maybe we should do a photo Christmas card." His earlier chuckles turned back into guffaws. "I can only imagine the look on his face when he opened it. His no-good half brother and his errant son living across the street from each other."

I couldn't stop myself. "We should add your mother into that picture."

He lost it. Once again, gales of laughter bounced off the walls. This time, I joined him.

It felt good to laugh.

CHAPTER ELEVEN

SEBASTIAN

Maggie had been quiet since we got back from Patrick and Eleanor's place. Patrick and I had talked more, and he told me to come back when I had time. He'd show me some pictures, and we could get to know each other more. I was looking forward to it.

Once we got home, Maggie made us some tea, and we sat on the couch, watching the snow that was beginning to fall.

"I've got some jobs to do for Eleanor starting Monday. I need to make a list of things to pick up." I sighed. "She insisted on giving me an advance so I could buy them."

"Is there a lot of work?"

I chuckled. "I think she likes to change things. I have a feeling it will be an unending process. Patrick says she loves to decorate and fix things. I think he's a very patient man." I grinned. "Who adores his wife."

Maggie hesitated. "How are you feeling about tonight? What you found out?"

I drew in a deep breath. "A lot of things. I'm furious with my father for lying all these years. I'm rather relieved I'm not the only person he has found lacking. I'm thrilled that I have a chance to know both Patrick and Eleanor." I set down my tea and turned to face Maggie fully. "And once again, I am so grateful for whatever divine being sent you in my direction."

Her eyes widened as I reached for her mug and set it on the table. I gathered her hands in mine. "Maggie, you have been an angel to me since I woke up and found you looking down at me. Because of you, I was brave enough to tell my father no. Because of you, I feel as if I have something to work toward in my life, and because of you, I found out I'm not as alone in this world as I thought I was."

"You have a new family," she whispered.

"Yes and no. You became my family the day you invited me into your life. Patrick and Eleanor are bonuses, but you're what matters. You are the most important thing to me."

I pulled her onto my lap, holding her close with my arm around her waist. I cupped her face. "You, me—*us*, Maggie. You're my life now."

"*Sebastian,*" she breathed. "I want to be yours."

"You are, Angel. All mine."

Yanking her tight to my chest, I captured her mouth with mine.

It was time.

I flicked off the light, then lifted her into my arms. Blindly, I carried her up the steps, my mouth never leaving hers. My shoulder glanced off the wall, my hip slammed into the handrail, and still, I refused to release her.

In our room, I lowered her to the mattress and stood back, looking at her bathed in the moonlight spilling through the window. She was a vision. Her russet-colored hair fanned over the white of the pillowcase. Her lips were full and pouty, beckoning my return. Her breasts were heaving under the long sweater she wore, the nipples taut and inviting my touch. She curled her fingers into fists, grasping the comforter in her want. Placing one knee on the mattress, I leaned forward, brushing my lips to hers. Her soft sigh was filled with need. I slid my fingers under the waistband of her leggings, pulling them down, exposing her shapely calves. I tugged off her socks, grinning at her wiggling toes. That was one of her signs of being nervous. I didn't want her nervous; I wanted her open and passionate. Lost in the same desire for me as I had for her.

I cupped the back of her neck, drawing her face to mine. I kissed her until she relaxed, her nerves gone and her desire raging.

"Let me see you, Maggie."

She didn't hesitate, pulling her sweater over her head. My breath caught in my throat as I gazed upon her body. Her skin was pale and luminous in the dim light, highlighted by the black lace of her lingerie. Slowly, I traced over the slim strap, fingering the lace. "So very beautiful, Angel. But this—" I dropped my hand to her waist, slipping my finger under the satin waistband "—and this, are hiding something far more beautiful. And I want it. I want you."

"Take me."

The pretty lace and satin didn't survive my eager hands. Shreds of both drifted to the floor until she was finally bare and visible to my lustful gaze. Her breasts fit in my hands perfectly. Her nipples were ready for my mouth, taut and sensitive as I teased and licked. I learned her body—the dips and hollows I discovered with my fingers and traced with my lips. By the time I was poised to take her, I knew how ticklish her knees were, how when I trailed my fingers over her hip bones, she shivered, and how she moaned deep in her throat when I nibbled the lobe of her ear and sucked at the skin behind it. She whimpered when I tasted her, my name falling from her lips as she rocked against my needy mouth. The insides of her thighs bore the signs of my teeth, and I branded her with a tiny purple mark at the base of her neck.

She found out how I loved her teeth teasing my nipples into tight peaks and the way I groaned as she pulled my hair in her passion. She traced the muscles in my back with her hands and tongue, and her mouth was wickedly talented when she drew my cock inside, using her tongue to tease, her teeth to excite, and her throat to swallow.

Hovering over her, I knew when I was finally enveloped in her warmth, when I could feel the heat and wetness of her desire, I would be complete. We'd already had the birth control and safety talk, so I knew we were covered. She was on birth control, and neither of us had been with anyone for a long time, so we were good. We would have nothing between us. With our fingers entwined and over her head, I thrust forward, my body pinning hers to the mattress, holding her captive under me. I cursed in pleasure at the feel of being joined with her, and she tightened her legs, drawing me closer. Our gazes locked as I began to move, her body bending, flowing in perfect symmetry with mine. My mouth covered hers as I moved more, taking her harder, not able to get close enough. I needed more. I wanted more. I wanted all of her. I wanted to be so deep inside her our bodies fused and melted together.

I continued to thrust into her until she screamed into my mouth, her pussy milking my cock as her muscles locked down and her orgasm raced through her. I kept moving, my own orgasm tearing through me, my balls tightening, pleasure snapping and rippling down my spine, through my body, and exploding in thousands of tiny shards of ecstasy.

Gradually, I stilled, reluctantly releasing her mouth from mine and separating our bodies. I lowered myself beside her, pulling her to me, unable to bear being apart from her.

I covered her face with kisses, our mouths meeting repeatedly—small, sweet gestures of affection and adoration. She smiled at me, sleepy, content, and sated.

"I'm falling in love with you, Sebastian," she whispered.

"Go ahead and fall, Angel," I murmured back. "I'll be there to catch you."

She tilted her head up, and I nuzzled her sweet mouth.

"Sleep, baby. I've got you."

She nestled closer and, within moments, was asleep.

I gazed down at her, marveling at the feelings she brought forth in me. She made me see things differently, want things I had never wanted before. I wanted to make this place a home for us. Build a life with her, have a family. I wanted to give our children something I never had—a caring father and a loving home. Maggie would be a wonderful mother; of that, I had no doubt.

I realized in that very moment that I was, in fact, already in love with her. I had probably loved her the very first moment I saw her leaning over me, protecting and caring for me in that airport.

I lowered my head and brushed my lips to her forehead. "I love you, Maggie," I breathed out. "And when you're ready, we're gonna be amazing."

Maggie was incredibly shy the next morning. I tried not to tease her, but I couldn't help it. She was far too adorable not to. She blushed and stammered as I stood at the end of our bed, tugging on the covers, telling her I wanted her in the shower with me. There was no question as to why I wanted her in there. My morning wood stood proud and happy to see her. We both wanted to see more of her, though, and we were looking forward to having her in the shower with us. The image of a wet and slippery Maggie, pressed against the cold tile while the heat of the shower created steam around us, was enticing. I wanted to be buried within her warmth again. I finally relented and went ahead of her, but I was waiting when she slipped into the bathroom. Her towel went over my shoulder, and I had her up on the vanity and my cock nestled to her entrance before she could even gasp. She was ready for me and climaxed so quickly, it caught me off guard. I slowed down, drawing out her pleasure and mine, until she was clawing at my back and begging me to take her harder.

I gave her what she wanted.

We didn't make it to the shower until much later.

And all it took was her washing my back for a repeat performance to occur.

I'd never been that clean in my life, and I was certain the shower had never seen the sorts of things that occurred in it that morning. Whatever the water bill was had been worth it.

I grinned at her over the rim of my mug. She glanced up and smiled, color flooding her cheeks. I couldn't help my laugh. "Really, Angel? After last night and this morning, I can still make you blush by grinning at you?"

"It's the way you're grinning."

"And how is that?"

"All proud and satisfied."

I took another drink of my coffee and nodded.

"Well, I suppose I am. I'm proud of myself for making you come last night…and this morning—twice, I might add. Nothing makes a man prouder than knowing his woman is fulfilled. And so, not only does that make me satisfied, I have to say, you were pretty fucking spectacular. So, I'm feeling rather fulfilled myself."

Her blush only deepened, which made me smile even harder. I stood, reaching over the table and grasping her neck, I kissed her hard. "You are amazing, Maggie. And you're all mine." I kissed her again. "Mine."

I sat back down, raising my mug, winking at her. She picked up her plate, carrying it to the sink, then turned, studying me as she lifted her mug.

"You were pretty spectacular yourself, Sebastian."

"I aim to please."

"You pleased."

"Good to know."

She set down her mug and walked to the doorway. "And just so we're clear?"

I raised my eyebrows in query.

"You're mine, too."

Those words did something to me. In a flash, I was out of my chair, chasing her up the stairs. I caught her at the top and flung her over my shoulder, carrying her back to our room.

"Gotcha!"

"I wasn't trying very hard."

I flung her down on the mattress, then pulled my shirt over my head.

"I'll show you hard, baby. So hard you'll scream."

She opened her arms. "I expect nothing less."

That was exactly what I gave her.

CHAPTER TWELVE

SEBASTIAN

I had no idea life could be as good as it was the next few months. Maggie and I settled into our new life together so easily, it was like breathing. She loved working at the library, and she was planning to start some courses online in the fall. I worked at the bar at night, and I had so many jobs waiting to be done, I was amazed. For a small town, the lack of knowledgeable handymen was surprising. Every time I spoke to Chris, I told him how much work there was here, hoping he would take the hint and come to check things out.

One weekend, the bar was fairly busy, but we had no sign-ups for the open mic night. Early in the evening, Maggie walked into the bar with a huge grin on her face, carrying my guitar case. Finn chuckled as he clapped me on the shoulder and informed me tonight was my night. I was so nervous, I actually shook when

I climbed up on that small stage. People were talking, laughing, drinking, and enjoying themselves. I wasn't sure they would even bother listening to me, and I thought about walking back off the stage and telling Finn to forget it.

Then my gaze found Maggie. She was sitting right in front, her hands clasped together in anticipation. She beamed at me, pride shining in her eyes. Beside her were Eleanor and Patrick; he grinned and gave me the thumbs-up. He and I had become very close the past while, and I considered him not only my uncle but my friend. Seeing the three people I cared about the most sitting, waiting for me, ready to support me, my nerves eased. I sat on the stool, adjusting the mic and strumming my guitar.

With a grin, I winked at Maggie and began to play. For the next thirty minutes, I lost myself in my music, playing song after song without a break, letting all my feelings flow through my fingers as they stroked my guitar, and my voice lifted, filling the bar. As the last notes died away, I was startled at the noise level, lifting my head and focusing on the room.

When had it filled up? And why was everyone on their feet?

I met Maggie's gaze, the tears glistening in her eyes as she stomped and clapped, yelling for an encore. Patrick's whooping and Eleanor's catcalls made me blush, and grasping the mic, I dropped my head down. Finn appeared beside me, patting me on the shoulder and handing me a cold drink.

"You have more, man? More songs?"

"Yeah." I nodded, almost draining the glass.

"Give them one more, and afterward, we need to talk about a regular night for you, my friend. You're gonna pack them in."

My face almost cracked from the width of my smile. I caught Maggie's eye again, giving her the thumbs-up. She was still clapping and calling out for me. I leaned closer to the mic. "Thanks, everyone. Really. I have one more for you." I paused, taking in a much-needed breath, finally saying the words I felt every single day. "This one is for my girl. The love of my life. Maggie, it's all because of you." I met her teary gaze steadily. "I love you, Angel."

She clasped her hands to her chest, allowing the tears to run down her cheeks. "I love you," she mouthed.

I began to play the song I'd written for her. The bar was full, the place becoming silent as I sang, but there was only her.

Only us.

I sang her the story of my love.

We were wrapped around each other as tight as possible. Not even a breath of air could slide between our heated bodies. After we'd left the bar and come home, we'd made love most of the night physically, while our voices spoke of it out loud. Hearing her say the words she had mouthed drove me to a frenzy, while mine were met with her sweet acceptance and gentle strength. I couldn't get enough of her, barely giving her time to sigh my name before I was on her again. The response to my music, to me, was like adrenaline to my body, and I was wound tighter than a spring.

The sun was already beginning its slow ascent when I finally pulled back, our sweat-soaked skin separating in a slow sound of protest. The stars were fading, giving way to morning, as I collapsed beside Maggie, tugging her close.

"Is that what always happens when you sing?" she asked, the question innocuous yet filled with an undercurrent.

"No," I assured her, pressing a kiss to her head. "Only when I sing for you."

"Okay, then." She sighed. "Sing away."

"Finn wants me to take over the Saturday night time slot. Every Saturday. He'll pay me extra for it so I'm not losing out on tips. He says he'll even pay me more if I draw in bigger crowds."

"That's awesome!"

I nodded. "He says I can do a few open mic nights too, if I want."

"Sebastian, that is so great." She enthused, pressing a kiss to my scruff. "I knew once he heard you, he would see how talented you are."

"You did this. You made all this happen." I waved my hand around the room. "You gave me a whole new life."

She buried her face into my neck, and I felt the heat of her blush. Slipping my hand under her chin, I lifted her face to mine. "I love you so much, Angel. I don't even have enough words to express it."

"I love my song."

"I have lots of songs inside to write for you."

She smiled, bending her face down and kissing my hand. "I already love them all."

I gathered her closer, wondering how I got so lucky. I knew every time I witnessed another snowstorm, I would remember the one that brought me to her. I pulled the blanket up over us. "Sleep, pretty girl. I've kept you up most of the night."

"Hmm… You did," she hummed. "We're going to sleep away most of the day."

"My father would find that wasteful."

"Your father can fuck off," she mumbled.

I burst out laughing, feeling her shake with mirth at her own words.

"Okay, Angel of mine with the foul mouth. Sleep."

I stood back, nodding in pride as I shoved my hammer into my tool belt. Eleanor's latest project was almost finished. The desk and built-in shelving unit in her "hobby room" were done. Tomorrow, I would paint them, add the trim, and the room would be complete. The new floor I installed was safe under the layer of plastic, and by the weekend, she would be busy crafting *stuff* in this room. I really had no idea what she'd be doing, but she was excited about it. So was Maggie, who I found out enjoyed "crafting" as well.

Who knew?

Eleanor appeared in the doorway, clapping her hands in glee as she opened the unit's doors and exclaimed her excitement over her rolling shelves and baskets I installed. The long cupboards with hanging rods were perfect for her fabrics and notions, she informed me. I grinned at her, having no idea what she was going on about, but happy I'd made what she wanted.

She threw her arms around me. "Thank you!"

I patted her back, still a little shy about her enthusiastic displays of affection. "You're welcome."

She pouted a little. "Mrs. Hammond's place is next?"

I laughed at her displeasure. "She's been waiting, Eleanor. I promised her kitchen reno would be done this month."

"But I'm next?"

I shook my head. "Your new steps will happen after Mrs. Adams's porch." I huffed a sigh. "Things will go faster when Chris gets here."

I really couldn't keep up. All I had accomplished at our place was to repair the sagging porch and fix the leak in the roof. I planned on a new one this summer and fixing up the outside, updating it a little. But I had no time at the moment.

"When does he arrive?"

"He should get here on Friday." I ran my hand over the back of my neck, the muscles sore after a long day. "I have to find out if he can stay over the bar for a while."

When Chris had told me he'd been laid off, I convinced him to come this way and give it a try. I knew he'd love it here, and the work was plentiful. He decided I was right—it was now or never, and he arranged to be here within a week. He sublet his furnished apartment to someone new, and he would be arriving much the same way I did—all his belongings in a suitcase and a few boxes. He was bringing his tools and his truck, which would make things much easier for us both when he got here.

Eleanor frowned. "I was thinking about that. Patrick and I wondered about offering him the room over the garage. It's basic but has its own bathroom. That way, he'd be close to you, and you could travel together."

"That's incredibly generous of you, Eleanor. You don't even know him. Are you sure?"

She nodded. "If he's a friend of yours, then it's good, Sebastian. He can pay us in trade." She winked. "I'm sure I have enough odd jobs around here, he can work off his room and board."

I threw back my head in laughter. "How easily I've been replaced."

She shook her head. "Nope. I will pay you for your work as always for the big jobs. But things like the creak in the stairs and the sticking windows upstairs? The boy can work for his dinner."

I kissed her cheek. "He'll be happy to, especially when he tastes your cooking. I'll warn you, though—the man is an endless pit. You'll be lucky if he doesn't eat you out of house and home."

"Duly noted." She clapped her hands. "Now, when are you going to do your kitchen?"

I huffed out a huge sigh. "I have everything but the countertop. I know what she wants. I just have to order it. I need to figure out a way of getting her away for a few days and surprising her. With Chris here, and Finn willing to help, we can knock it out in a day and rebuild in three. I'll move the one wall for the laundry room behind it the way I planned, but the rest is easy."

"Patrick wants to help."

"Um…"

She laughed at my expression. He was terrible when it came to home renos. "Maybe you can put him on errand and trash detail. Barbecuing the meals."

I chuckled. He did barbecue well. "That works."

"There's a craft show in Calgary in two weeks. It's a two-day event. I could take Maggie and add in a play or something. We'll visit Connie, too. We could leave on Thursday morning, and I can drag it out until Monday night. Maybe even Tuesday if I invent a side trip on the way home. Would that work?"

I nodded eagerly. "That would be amazing."

"Okay, I'll bring it up at dinner. You act surprised and supportive. I'll handle the rest."

I beamed at her. "Sounds like a plan. Thank you, Eleanor."

She patted my cheek. "That's what families do, Sebastian. Help one another."

I smiled, feeling grateful, as I watched her leave the room.

It was great to have a family.

I walked into the bar on Thursday to a spectacle playing out for all to see—Chris, on his knees, begging the "fair Mandy" to marry him. She was another server here and had become a good friend to Maggie. I liked her a lot.

I met Mandy's somewhat confused, but not-quite-pissed gaze with a smirk.

"He belong to you?" she asked.

Before I could answer, he was on his feet, swinging himself around, his arms spread wide. "Sebastian, my man!"

I took a step back in shock. How was it possible he'd gotten even larger than the last time I saw him? His arms resembled tree trunks, and he wrapped them around me, lifting me from my feet and squeezing all the air from my lungs.

"I've been waiting for you!"

I gasped for air after he set me down on the floor. Then he slapped my back so hard, I had to grab the nearest chair in order not to fall flat on my face.

Chris, of course, laughed. "I forgot what a girlie man you were."

I shook my head, unable to help the grin on my face. "Listen, you idiot, I told these people you were a nice guy! You're screwing it all up."

He grinned back at me. "Nah. Finn and I are already friends, and Amber loves me! I used her earlier for some arm curls—she's perfect!" He threw Mandy a wink. "And once the fair Mandy agrees to marry me, I am all set!"

The image of Amber clutching his arm while he chatted with Finn and lifted her up and down made me laugh. Only Chris.

"You were supposed to arrive tomorrow."

"I made good time."

"You did." I slapped his shoulder, grimacing at the solid piece of granite under my palm. "I'll call Maggie and let her know you've arrived. She's coming over later."

He smiled so widely, his dimples had dimples in them. "I can hardly wait to meet her."

Amber piped up as she came out of the kitchen. "You can use her for your other arm, Chris."

He beamed. "Perfect!"

It was a lively crew that hung around the bar that night. Patrick and Eleanor came over with Maggie, and they sat around with Chris until closing. Once we could join them, we all relaxed, drinking, eating, and talking. I looked around, feeling a sense of rightness. Patrick and Eleanor were like proud parents, smiling at all of us. Finn had Amber tucked beside him, laughing at something she said, Chris was charming Mandy, who was being unusually giggly, and Maggie was quiet but happy as she gazed at everyone. I caught her gaze and bent low, brushing a kiss across her cheek to her ear.

"Feels like we've created our own family, yes?"

She nodded.

Eleanor spoke up. "Chris, your room is all set, so you can follow us back to the house when you're ready."

"You're too kind."

I laughed. "She has a list of jobs for you, trust me. The one thing that doesn't ever change in Eleanor's house is the list of changes she wants to make!"

Everyone chuckled, even as she cuffed the back of my head. "Careful, Sebastian. Chris might become my favorite."

Chris cracked his knuckles. "No might about it. I will be for sure!"

There was more laughter and lots of good-natured ribbing before we broke up for the night. When we arrived home, Maggie went inside, while I went across the street and helped Chris carry his bags up to his room. He looked around with a low whistle.

"This is bigger than my whole apartment in Toronto."

"I know. It's on Eleanor's list—she wants to fix it up more, but you'll be comfortable. And she's a fantastic cook."

"I can't stay here for nothing, Sebastian." He ran his hand over the back of his neck. "You know what I eat."

"I'll leave that between you and Eleanor. I'm sure you'll work it out."

"So, he's your uncle, eh?"

"Half uncle, yes. I'd call him a friend first, I think."

He became serious for a moment. "Thank you for this, Sebastian. When I was laid off, I had no idea what I was going to do. Jobs are hard to find right now."

"I know. I have more work here than I can handle, and we have worked so well together in the past. I think you'll like it here."

"I think I will. So, Mandy… She isn't taken, is she?"

"No. She had a bad experience, and she's pretty gun-shy, apparently. She was married, and the divorce was nasty. He was some piece of work from what I gather."

"He still around?"

"No, he moved. Once people found out how he treated her and they rallied around her, he was pretty quick to take off."

"Asshole."

"Yep. But she is great. She and Maggie have been getting closer. She's cautious, though."

He nodded. "I can work with that. She's spectacular." He winked at me. "So is your little airport angel."

"That is an understatement. Maggie is…*everything*."

"You look happy."

"I am—more than I ever expected to be."

"Have you heard from your dad?"

I felt a small twinge of sadness. "No. I wrote him twice, but he hasn't written back. He ignores my voice mails too. His secretary just says he's unavailable when I call."

"Sorry, man."

I shrugged. "His choice, not mine. I found something here, Chris. I feel as if this is where I was meant to be. I enjoy working, I get to play in the bar, I have new friends, Patrick, Eleanor, and…" My voice trailed off, my throat becoming thick for some reason.

"Maggie," he finished for me, nodding. "She's perfect for you."

"She is."

"You found your life."

I held out my hand. "I hope you find yours here, too."

He ignored my hand, dragging me in for another one of his bear hugs. "Me too."

The next few days were crazy—and awesome. Between the bar and the list of people waiting for jobs to be done, I was constantly on the go. Chris and I picked up our relationship both personally and professionally without a hitch. Maggie was a wonder, working on our schedules and looking after invoices.

During dinner at Eleanor's on Wednesday, I looked over the calendar she had done up.

"We are booked solid."

Chris beamed around a mouthful of potatoes. "It's great."

Maggie frowned. "The only thing I'm not sure of is this Bird sink install next weekend. I can't find anything about it in your notes, Sebastian."

I shoveled in a mouthful of chicken, trying to buy some time. Eleanor spoke up. "Oh, never mind about a job for them that weekend, Maggie! There's a craft fair in Calgary I am dying to go to, and Patrick can't take the time off. If Sebastian is booked, will you go with me?"

Maggie's eyes lit up. "A craft fair?"

Eleanor nodded. "It's huge. And *Mousetrap* is playing at one of my favorite little theatres. We'll take Connie with us to see it. We can make it a long weekend!"

Maggie looked worried. "I'd have to ask at the library for the time off, although I'm sure it's fine, but…" She trailed off, her voice sounding uncertain, and she looked at me.

I leaned forward, brushing her hair over her shoulder. "First off, Angel, you don't need my permission. Second, Eleanor is right. I have an install I promised to help with, so I'll be busy all weekend. If you can get the time off, go and enjoy yourself." I already knew she could since I had called her boss and told him what I had planned. I had already done some work for him and he planned to use me again, so he was more than fine with her taking a couple of days off. I made him promise to act as if he knew nothing when she inquired. I pressed a kiss to her cheek. "I'll miss you, but I want you to go and have fun. Buy some crafty things for our home. Give Connie a hug and tell her I look forward to seeing her again soon." She had come to town after Patrick called her, and he was right. His mother was warm, friendly, and loving. We got along well and kept in touch regularly.

She beamed at me. "Okay."

I sat back, hiding my grin. She had no idea. She was going to be so surprised.

Perfect.

The minute the coast was clear, we started. Amber and Mandy came over and helped us pack up the cupboards. I had done a bunch the day before, taking Maggie out for dinner and keeping her out of the kitchen so she didn't notice the empty cupboards. It had been easy to distract her when we got back—I helped her pack then made love to her until she fell asleep. This morning, I had coffee ready for her and woke her up just in time to grab a shower and be ready when Eleanor arrived.

By noon, the kitchen was empty, and the old washer and dryer gone. The electrician was already wiring up a new outlet for where I was moving the newer stacking appliances I had bought for Maggie that had been hiding in Eleanor's garage, along with all the other supplies. They were my biggest splurge, but the old ones were in pretty bad shape, and the new stacking set fit so much better.

We worked tirelessly, Finn being kind enough to have my two shifts covered at the bar. I promised to make it up with an extra set in the future. He was pleased since the crowds grew every time I performed, so the bar did well.

By Sunday night, the flooring was down, cupboards installed, the rooms painted, and we were busy in the newly converted laundry/bathroom. Monday, the countertops would go in both rooms, I would add the hardware, and the new-to-us appliances would be hooked up. Maggie was going to flip. Eleanor had decided she "needed" new ones and insisted I take her old ones. I knew from Patrick she had only bought them a year ago, but she claimed she wanted stainless and her white ones *had* to go. He just grinned and clapped me on the shoulder. "Let her do this, Sebastian. She adores Maggie. Both of you, actually. I don't care if she buys a new set every month if it makes her happy."

Once again, I was left reeling from their generosity. How I had gotten so lucky, I didn't know. But since meeting Maggie, my life had changed, and all for the better.

Monday night, I looked around, pleased. The cupboards were painted a soft dove gray, the counters a blend of silver, gray, and white quartz Maggie had drooled over when I took her to look at samples for "another customer," and the floor a dark gray slate. Eleanor's appliances included a dishwasher, which Maggie had never had before now, and I knew she was going to love the refrigerator with the French doors and the self-cleaning oven. The bathroom was simple, but it would be a useful feature, saving lots of trips up and down the stairs, especially when we had guests.

Chris clapped me on the shoulder. "We did good. This looks great."

"It does. I feel like I'm leaving a lot of work for Maggie to put things back in cupboards, though."

He shook his head. "Nope. The girls are right—she'll want to pick where things go. I'll come help when she decides." He nudged me in the ribs. "She's gonna be busy with the thank-yous for a bit."

I shook my head even as I bit back my grin. I had missed her terribly. I missed the sound of her voice, her teasing laughter, and the way she nestled into me at night. I missed making love to her before going to sleep, and waking up without her beside me felt lonely and odd. I wanted her home.

"You're so going to marry this girl, aren't you?"

"Yep."

"You plan on staying here? No more wanderlust or chasing a music career?"

I rubbed my chin thoughtfully. "Maggie asked me the same thing one day. I had that, Chris. I lived in a big city, surrounded by people and things. I was invisible—I wasn't happy. I loved playing music, but all the BS that went along with it? Hated it. Here, people wave and know my name. I can breathe. I feel welcome. And what we're doing? Our construction business? Some people, like my father, would find it beneath them—considering it grunt labor. But I like it. I get to work with my best friend every day."

He grinned widely at my words. "I know. I'm pretty great."

I chuckled, then became serious. "I get to play my music, so I still have it. I have everything I never knew I was searching for right here. Most importantly, I have Maggie. Wherever she is, is where I will be. For the rest of my life, I want to be with her." I blew out a long breath, trying to find the right words. "I feel as if I've come home now. She is my home." I shook my head. "It's been a long time since I felt that way."

"I get that."

"We can build a life here. A simple one to some people, but to me, it's exactly what I want."

"I'm happy for you."

"How's it going with the fair Mandy?"

"Slow." He smiled, but his eyes were soft. "But she is going to be worth it—I can tell."

"Then I guess we're set."

"Yep."

He waved as he left, hurrying back to Eleanor and Patrick's. He and Patrick were planning on surprising her with dinner for when she got home. The two of them loved to use the outdoor grill as much as possible.

I smiled, thinking about the conversation. I had a wonderful life here. Maggie made it wonderful. And I hoped what I had done in her house—our house—made her happy.

Headlights flashed across the window, and I stood from my chair.

I guessed it was time to find out.

CHAPTER THIRTEEN

SEBASTIAN

Maggie never made it past the steps before I had the door flung open and her wrapped in my arms. I held her tight, dropping my face to her neck, breathing in her scent. She huffed out a long exhale of air, her body relaxing into my embrace. I bent and grabbed the small bag she had dropped, stepped back into the house, kicking the door shut behind me. My lips sought hers, and I kissed her deeply. Moments passed as I savored the feel of her mouth under my lips.

"Fuck, Angel, I missed you," I groaned.

She smiled up at me, her eyes wide, face beaming. "If that's how you are going to greet me, I may have to go away more often."

"No. No more trips for a while. I missed you too much."

Reaching up, she stroked my cheek with her fingers. "Okay. I missed you too."

"Yeah?"

"Very much."

"But you had a good time with Eleanor?"

"I did. It was amazing."

"I don't see any bags."

"They're all in her trunk. We have to sort it out tomorrow, and I'll bring my stuff home then." Color collected under her skin, and she smiled shyly. "I think she knew how anxious I was to see you."

"Smart woman."

"Did you get everything done while I was gone? You didn't work all weekend, did you? Did you eat?"

I set her down with a grin. Her need to look after me was still so new and amazing.

"Yes."

"Your customers were all happy?"

I sucked in a deep breath. "Well, you'll have to tell me."

"What?"

I held out my hand, nerves kicking in. It was showtime. "Come with me."

I didn't know what I expected when Maggie saw what I had done. I'd hoped she would like it. I wanted to see the joy on her face when she saw her new kitchen.

What I didn't expect were the tears.

She stood in the middle of the room, her hand over her mouth as she turned in a circle, not making a sound. She did that twice, then walked over to the new counters, ran a finger along the smooth surface, reached up, opening a cupboard door, letting it close on its own.

"I added the soft close feature," I spoke up. "I thought you'd like that."

Silence.

She stepped over to the stove, studying it.

"Eleanor gave us her appliances. They're only a year old, still like new," I offered, shifting on my feet, feeling nervous.

Why wasn't she saying anything?

It suddenly occurred to me maybe I had overstepped. I thought I knew what Maggie wanted. I thought she'd be thrilled, but maybe I had been wrong. Maybe this was something she wanted to do herself. Perhaps reconditioned cupboards and used appliances weren't what she wanted at all, no matter how nice they were. Maybe I had just fucked everything up.

"Maggie, Angel…if you hate it—"

She held up her hand and turned to look at me. Tears poured down her face.

Fuck. She was upset.

"Maggie—"

"How?" she choked out.

"What?"

"How did you do all this, Sebastian?" She touched the counter. "This is the pattern I fell in love with." Her gaze drifted to the cupboards. "The handles I admired in the hardware store."

"I know. I wanted to give you everything you liked. I've been buying things as I found them and storing them in Eleanor's garage. She gave me some of the cupboards when I replaced hers, and I bought the others." I swallowed. "Are you angry?"

"Angry?" She hiccupped.

"That I did this without your permission? Renovated your house?"

She shook her head wildly. "*Our* house."

Those words warmed my chest. I stepped forward, completely confused. "Why are you crying?"

"Why did you do these renovations?"

I smiled. "Because I love you, and you wanted a pretty kitchen. I tried to give you that wish."

"No one has ever done anything like this for me."

"No one deserves it more. It's my way of saying thank you."

She lunged forward, and I caught her in my arms. Her shoulders shook with the force of her sobs, which I now understood to be happy, yet somewhat confused tears. I held her close, shushing her and stroking her hair.

"It's the most beautiful kitchen I have ever seen!" she exclaimed between sobs. "I can't believe you did all this for me! How–how did you do all this in one weekend?"

"I had help. Chris, Finn, and Patrick all pitched in. Mandy and Amber packed up everything."

"They all knew?"

I smirked, wiping the tears off her cheeks. "Eleanor organized it all. She took you away so I could do this for you."

More tears welled in her eyes.

"Enough crying. You're supposed to be happy," I chided her gently. I hated seeing her cry.

"I am. I'm just overwhelmed. I can't believe you did this for me. I can't believe you love me enough to do —" she waved her arm "—all this work." She gazed up at me. "No one has over loved me that much."

I bent down, brushing her lips with mine. "Ditto. You give me so much. This was just a start to my thank-you for what you have done for me. The way you have made my life so much better than I ever imagined it could be."

She flung her arms around my neck, holding me tight. I held her to my chest, smiling as she whispered, "Oh my God, Sebastian, is that a *dishwasher*?"

Setting her down, I chuckled. "Let me show you your new kitchen, Angel. Then you can check out the new laundry room and guest bathroom."

She let out a squeal that made me laugh. That was what I wanted.

Maggie's happiness.

***

We sat at the table, eating some snacks I had picked up—or, rather, I was. Maggie kept standing, opening cupboards, touching the counter, and smiling. She would sit down, beam at me, sip her wine, and start the whole process over again. At times, she'd disappear into the new laundry/bath area, returning with a grin. Finally, I pulled her to my lap, winding my arm around her waist.

"Stay." I laughed. "I've missed you so much, and you keep disappearing on me."

"Every time I look, I see something new. Everything is so pretty. It all looks like me—exactly what I would pick out. Like you stepped into my brain and took all the ideas out and, bam! There they are!" she rambled. "I'm just so overwhelmed!" She ran her finger along the thick wooden table. "This is so beautiful. I love the grain and the color. I just love everything."

I grinned since that was the Maggie I knew. Excited and talking.

"Chris made it with some planks we pulled out of that farmhouse a few weeks ago. I knew how much you wanted a big table for in here. He left them weathered and just varnished them." I pulled at the end. "It opens up so you can get more people around it."

"I am so hosting Thanksgiving."

"We'll need more chairs." I had kept the two Maggie had, but that was all we owned. "I bet Chris could make some simple ones we could paint white."

She nodded. "I would love that. I can make some pretty cushions to go on the chairs. Eleanor and I will do it in her hobby room. She'll love it."

"You do that. I'll talk to Chris. He loves making things in his downtime. I'll get six done."

She counted off on her fingers. "Eight."

I leaned forward, kissing the soft spot behind her ear that made her shiver. "Maybe ten, yes? We can store them in the basement, and one day, we may need them for when we have kids, plus our crew here."

Her eyes widened, and I held my breath. Then she smiled. That smile I loved the best. Wide, excited, and filled with love.

"Yes. For our kids."

I crashed my mouth to hers, holding her tight. Her fingers tightened on my neck, and she moaned low in her throat as our tongues stroked together.

"Have you seen enough of your kitchen, Maggie? How about I take you upstairs and show you how much I missed you?"

Her hand snaked between us, cupping my growing erection. "Yes, Sebastian. Take me upstairs and welcome me home."

I stood, setting her on her feet. "I'll make sure everything's locked up. Be waiting for me. *Naked.*"

Climbing the stairs, I could see the glow of candlelight flickering on the walls. Maggie enjoyed making love by candlelight. I loved watching the way her skin glowed and the light danced over her face when she was coming around me. Walking into the room, I paused at the door. She was gloriously naked. Her hair was a burnished halo in the soft glow as she lay on the white sheets, one hand curled under her cheek, waiting for me. I gazed upon her beautiful form—the nuances of her small body still fresh to me. I discovered something new to fall in love with every time I touched her. A secret ticklish spot, the way she would moan when my lips found a hidden dip to taste, an undiscovered freckle to bathe with my tongue.

I pulled my shirt over my head, yanking off my sweats, and climbed on the mattress, unable to be away from her a second longer. I settled between her legs, balancing my weight on my forearms as I captured her mouth, kissing her passionately. She wrapped her legs around me, her arms folding around my torso, welcoming me home to the cradle of her body. Long moments passed as we kissed, murmurs of love and longing passing between us. Slowly, we explored each other, our hands and mouths caressing, touching, rediscovering.

"No more trips for a while," I rasped against her skin. "I need you here with me."

"Okay," she agreed, pulling my mouth back to hers.

Passion built, our bodies moving and aligning. I sank into her heat, groaning at the feeling of being joined with her again. "Every time, Angel. It feels like the first time, every damn time."

"Sebastian," she breathed out, her hands tightening on my skin. "*Please*, baby."

I loved it when she called me baby. She only did it in the most intimate moments; the sound of the word uttered in that low, breathless voice always cranked me even higher.

I pressed her hands over her head, our fingers entwined, thrusting into her as deeply as I could. She arched up to meet me, her cries and whimpers stirring my lust. I kissed her damp skin, flicking my tongue over the softness, returning to her mouth. Heat slithered down my spine, my orgasm growing in the pit of my stomach, my balls tightening with my impending climax.

"Come for me, Angel. I need you with me."

She cried out, her head lifting as she shouted my name. Burying my head into her neck, I breathed out her name, moving inside her until I was spent. Stilling, I rolled, taking her with me, holding her tight.

"I love you."

She snuggled closer, her hand resting over my heart.

"I love you."

CHAPTER FOURTEEN

MAGGIE

I walked into the bar, greeting people, smiling. Near the small stage, Patrick and Eleanor waited at our usual table. He had his arm draped over the back of her chair and was listening intently to something she said. We had grown so close to them since arriving in Riverstoke. So much of our life revolved around them and our friends who had become our family.

I had been so unsure about returning to Riverstoke. When my dad was alive, it felt like home—once he had passed, I wasn't sure how I would feel coming back. I was searching for something. A place to belong. I didn't know if I would find it coming back here. But I did.

I found that place with a man who was searching for his own spot in the world. Together, Sebastian and I made a life. With him beside me, Riverstoke was home again. The place I would always return to, knowing I belonged. The people were warm and friendly. They welcomed me back and accepted him completely. This small community was where we wanted to stay and bring up our kids.

Amber appeared beside me, hooking her arm with mine. "He's been looking for you."

I laughed. "It was activity day at the library. I had glitter and glue in my hair. I needed to shower and change." I shook my head. "How can he still be nervous? He's up there a lot. The stage is a second home to him."

"He's humble that way."

"I'll go see him."

Sebastian was leaning across the bar, talking to Finn. The sight of him made my heart flutter. Tall and strong, his shirt stretched across his biceps, hard and thick from his manual labor, he was incredibly sexy. I knew all the single women, and most of the married ones, in town agreed with me. He and Chris were known as the dynamic duo of handymen, and their services were in great demand. He packed the bar on Saturday nights, plus any other time he stepped onstage. But as Amber said, he was still humble.

He turned, spotting me, his face breaking out into a wide smile. His pleasure at seeing me did something to my chest, warming me instantly. There was no doubt of his feelings for me—they were on full display for anyone to witness. They filled his music, his lyrics humming with emotion.

He crossed the bar, moving through the crowd to get to me, sliding his arm around my waist and tugging me close.

"Hey, Angel. I was hoping you'd get here soon."

Then he kissed me, ignoring the catcalls and whoops —the loudest from Patrick. Sebastian grinned, dropping another kiss to my cheek.

"I love, after all this time, you still blush for me," he murmured.

"Everyone is looking."

He chuckled. "Let them look. I'm proud to show off my love for my girl." He tugged me over to the table. "I've got some news."

I sat down, looking at Patrick and Eleanor. They were as curious as I was, so he obviously hadn't shared yet.

I pulled off my coat. "What?"

"Remember the guy who was in here last week? The suit I thought looked out of place?"

I nodded. He had rich businessman written all over him—not the sort you found in Riverstoke on a Saturday night, sitting in a bar having a beer.

"He represents a singer." Sebastian's eyes danced as he named a well-known artist. "He wants to buy some of my songs and sing them."

I flung my arms around his neck. "That is amazing!"

He looked excited. "I met with both of them today via Zoom. I would still own my stuff, but he would sing it. I get paid up front, plus royalties."

He glanced at Patrick. "I'm going to need a lawyer. I know nothing about this stuff."

Patrick grinned. "I can help you there. I know several."

"Great." Sebastian ran a hand through his hair, looking unusually flustered. "I mean, it might go nowhere—"

I cut him off. "It won't. He's huge. He'll want more of your songs." I frowned. "Will you have to leave?"

"Only for a day or two at a time, if anything. To meet him. Help with musical arrangements." He grabbed my hand and kissed it. "This could be the break I wanted. I can write my music and hear it on the radio. Perform other stuff here. Live my life—with you. The best of both worlds."

"Is it enough?" I asked, worried. He had dreamed of bigger things.

He looked shocked at my question, but before he could answer, Finn called him to the stage. He stood, cupped my face, and kissed me. He met my worried gaze. "Yes," he said firmly. "It is enough. As long as you're part of the equation, it will *always* be enough."

Then he strode to the stage, smiling and happy. Patrick leaned over, meeting my eyes.

"He has everything he wants here, Maggie. Never doubt that. He loves you beyond reason. He's happy —something I don't think he's been for a very long time. Trust that. Trust him."

I met Sebastian's eyes. As usual, they were focused on me. I smiled at him, blowing him a kiss. Patrick was right. Sebastian was happy. His light had been dimmed when I met him, as he searched for his place, lost and alone. Now, he burned bright, his creativity high. He wrote at all hours, often making Chris laugh when he would scribble lyrics on a wall or a piece of wood that was handy. His phone was full of pictures of lyrics, notes, jotted ideas. His customers had no idea of the imaginative works hidden under their paint or moldings. I loved the fact that I was often the inspiration, but he found ideas everywhere. The sound of the wind, a word or scent that stirred a memory for him. He was filled with music. With love and a zest for life. He filled me with the same passion.

Together, we were strong.

We walked home from the bar, the cool of the autumn air beginning to close in around us. I shivered, and Sebastian tugged me closer. He paused as we reached the house, looking at it from the road. The porch no longer leaned, and the roofline was once again straight and even, with new shingles and no leaks. He and Chris had pulled down the porch and rebuilt it, adding cedar columns, railings, and a swing for me to sit in. We had painted the faded siding a deep blue and added black shutters. It looked updated, clean, and homey. Eleanor and I planned on working on the garden next year, and I was excited thinking about decorating the house for Christmas. Putting up lights outside, a tree in the living room.

Our first Christmas together.

I glanced up at Sebastian. He was studying me with an intensity that was disconcerting.

"What?" I asked.

He set down his guitar case. "That house represents so much to me, Maggie."

"You've put a lot of work into it."

"Aside from that. It represents safety. Acceptance. Love. I got all that from you the day I met you. It all grew into something even bigger in that house. The house grew into a home, the town became not just the place I live, but the hometown I always wanted. All because of you. Your trust." He ran a finger down my cheek. "Your love."

I smiled, feeling the tears building. "You did the same for me, Sebastian. You made coming back here coming home. *You* are my home."

"Tell me you know it's enough. That you will always be enough. If I had nothing else but you, this little house, and the life we have together, it would still be all I want. If I get to sell my music, that's just an added bonus. The dreams I had of making it big, walking onstage to thousands of fans, they were just that—a dream. One I no longer need."

"Why? What changed?"

He shrugged self-consciously. "Part of it was to prove to my dad I wasn't the failure he said I was. I don't have to prove anything anymore, because in your eyes, I'm not that."

"You never were. Your dad was wrong."

"Your belief in me astounds me. It always will." He smiled. "I was sort of hoping maybe you might promise to remind me of that belief—" he swallowed, looking nervous "—for the rest of your life? Let me follow you wherever you go, Maggie. Because where you are is home."

My breath caught in my throat. Sebastian lowered himself to one knee and offered me a small box. "It's not much, my Angel, but it would make me the happiest man in the world if you would wear this ring and agree to marry me."

I covered my mouth, tears gathering in my eyes. I could only nod as Sebastian beamed, standing and wrapping me in his arms. I sobbed out his name, and he hugged me close.

"You shouldn't be crying, Maggie. You haven't seen the ring yet."

I stepped back, laughing at his drollness. I didn't need to see the ring. All I wanted was him. Still, he opened the box, showing me the delicate ring inside. The emerald twinkled in the overhead streetlights, the tiny diamonds around it flashing their brilliance.

"Mr. Archer, the jeweler, said not every engagement ring is a diamond. I thought you might like this one since you always say you love my eyes. But we can exchange—"

I cut him off. "It's perfect."

He slipped it on my finger and kissed my hand. "So are you."

"I'll remind you of that in a few years."

He bent and kissed me. "You do that, Angel. You do that."

CHAPTER FIFTEEN

SEBASTIAN

I strummed my guitar, getting ready to head to the stage. It was a full house tonight, and the front table held the people I cared about the most. I hadn't played in a couple of weeks, having been busy with negotiations to sell some of my music. I'd had to fly to Toronto to attend a few meetings. I was glad to be back in this small place, the quiet and slower pace far more suited to my head than the craziness Toronto held. Tomorrow was Thanksgiving, and I knew Eleanor and Maggie had been cooking up a storm for the meal. Tonight, I would celebrate my contract, my music, and being home.

I stepped on the stage, smiling good-naturedly at the applause. I'd played a few songs, enjoying the interaction with the crowd, when I saw him.

My father was there. Sitting at the edge of the bar, scowling at me. I never expected to see him here, of all places, and my smile slipped from my face before I could stop it. I quickly forced it back, bending my head to strum a little and gather my wits. When I glanced up again, his distaste was evident on his face. I was immediately both angry and wary.

Why was he there?

Maggie saw the look on my face, and, glancing around, her gaze found my father. She leaned over and spoke quietly to Patrick, who turned and met my father's gaze. The disgust on his face became anger when he saw Patrick as well as his mother, Connie, who was visiting that weekend. She was a regular visitor to Riverstoke and part of our small circle of adopted family. I adored her and loved hearing stories about my grandfather.

I ended my set early, stood, and I approached my father, knowing many eyes were on us.

He looked the same as he always did—his posture rigid, shoulders set, and his demeanor cold. Although Patrick did look like Connie, I saw a slight resemblance between him and my father, but whereas Patrick was warmth personified, my father was icy and cold. I tried to remember kind-heartedness or caring, but instead, I only remembered his distance. I was surprised to find the longing for his approval gone, and in its place, complete indifference.

I nodded at him. "Father."

"I see nothing's changed. Still wasting your life chasing a dream."

I shook my head in disagreement. "A lot has changed. You can't be bothered to see it, and frankly, I don't feel like sharing. How did you find me?"

"The postmark on one of the letters you sent. It wasn't hard."

"Why are you here?"

"I am done being patient. It is time for you to return to Vancouver."

I gaped at him. "You can't show up here and order me around like an errant little boy. I am not returning to Vancouver. This is my home."

"Don't be ridiculous."

"I think you're the ridiculous one here. You arrive and demand I leave? You have no right."

"I'm your father. Your blood."

I clutched the back of my neck, feeling my tension ramping up. "Yes, you are my father. But you threw away any chance of that meaning something when you chose to ignore me for the past months. Just like you ignored me my whole life." I crossed my arms, meeting his gaze. "Family is more than blood. It's caring, love, and support."

I sucked in a deep breath. "My family is here. If you can be civil, you are welcome to join us for a drink."

"I will not sit down at a table with those people."

"Then you can leave."

"You would choose them over me?"

I barked out a laugh. "You chose work over me. Strangers meant more to you than I ever did. You ignored me for years and belittled everything I loved. Your opinions and feelings no longer matter."

He slid off his chair and stepped forward, his eyes narrowed. "You owe me a great deal of money. You are coming with me and working it off."

For the first time, I noticed his speech. It wasn't as smooth as usual. As he came closer, I realized he had been drinking. I always hated it when he drank. He was never a violent person, but after he had a few drinks in him, his tongue became exceptionally sharp. I needed him to say what he had to say and leave before he caused a scene.

"I'm not going anywhere. I asked you to tell me what I owed in my letters, which, obviously, you didn't bother to read. Tell me how much, and I will repay you as quickly as I can." I knew he wanted to be reimbursed for the plane fare and the money he'd sent me. I wondered what else he wanted returned.

"I want it now."

"I don't have it." I hadn't received the advance in my contract yet, but it was coming.

"You never will."

"Yes, I will." I had no desire to share with him why I could repay him. He would only mock it, and I refused to allow him to do so.

"We'll figure it out together." Maggie appeared in front of me. She reached behind, grasping my hand. "I don't like the tone you're speaking to my fiancé with. I would like you to leave."

"Fiancé, now? What a loser. Frankly, you stupid girl, I don't care what you say. He is coming with me, and he can work off his debt. Once he's done, let's see how fast you take him back."

She crossed her arms, pissed. "I will *always* take him back, but he isn't going anywhere! Certainly not with the likes of you. Who do you think you are, coming in here and making demands? You haven't spoken to your son in months or returned his messages. You upset him terribly," she insisted, her words coming out fast. "You should be ashamed of yourself. All he wants is your approval and your love. He deserves that. Sperm doesn't make you a father. It's your actions that do." She was so angry, I was certain she was about to stomp her foot. "He is a good man. Kind. Loving. Talented. You should be proud." She shook her head in frustration, her hands curled into fists. "You blind, mean…jackass!" she hurled at him.

My father stared at her, not paying any attention to her heartfelt words. He reached past Maggie to seize my arm. With a gasp, she grabbed his hand, stopping him. His temper erupted, and he pushed her to the side, causing her to stumble. She hit the table behind her, her arms flailing. Patrick and I grasped for her before she hit the floor, both of us livid.

"You bastard!" I yelled, wrapping her close. All hell broke loose. Chris had my father in a headlock, and Patrick was standing in front of Maggie and me protectively. Finn cleared the bar in a huge jump, grabbing his phone, ready to call the police. The entire place watched as my father glared at us but didn't make another move.

"Let him go, Chris," Patrick spoke up, his voice stern. He directed his anger at my father. "You make one more move toward either of them, you'll be sorry."

My father straightened up. "How surprising. One slacker defending another. How the two of you got together, I have no idea, but good riddance. You've obviously had a bad influence on Sebastian."

Patrick laughed. "Whatever. Whoever you want to blame, go ahead. God knows you can't blame yourself."

My father pointed a finger at me. "You owe me."

"Leave the boy alone. Whatever it is, I'll pay it. Give me a figure, and I'll write you a check," Patrick spat out.

I gaped at him. So did my father. Then he recovered.

"Having your friends paying off your debts now, Sebastian?" He sneered. "I'm not sure you can afford it, Patrick. He has quite a large debt."

Patrick laughed. "First off, he is more than a friend. You damn well know that. Sebastian is family. We take care of our family here. And I know he's good for it. He's one of the most trustworthy people I know. The fact that you can't, or won't, see that in your own son is just sad." He gave my father a look that spoke volumes. "Shame his—" he raised his hands, making quotation marks in the air "—'real family' refuses to accept or see him for the amazing young man he is." Then he smirked. "As for affording it, I can assure you, I could buy and sell you ten times over. Trust me on that one."

Connie joined our group. "I'll pay whatever bill you send." Her voice was low, her words frank. "Your father would be ashamed of you."

My father stepped forward menacingly. "I don't give a—"

Patrick stepped in front of him. "Don't you dare. You speak to my mother with respect, or you keep your mouth shut. And you keep your hands to yourself, or

I'll teach you a lesson you've needed for a very long time."

"You wouldn't. I'll bring you up on charges."

"The police chief is right over there." I pointed to the corner. "He'd testify we were protecting my grandmother and my fiancée."

His eyes narrowed, and he glanced over his shoulder. Tom nodded in affirmation of my words. My father finally realized he was surrounded by people against him. I had seen the way his shoulders tensed when I called Connie my grandmother. He didn't like it, but I no longer cared.

He blanched, then shook off the hand Chris still had on his shoulder. "I'll send you an invoice. I don't care who pays it as long as I get my money." He shook his head. "You'll never get a penny back. The boy will never amount to anything."

Patrick nodded. "That's where you're wrong. He is already more than you will ever know. More than you will ever be. You should be proud, but you're too blind to see it. Too prideful to admit you're wrong. You always have been."

I felt my chest warm at his words.

My father looked around the room, taking note of all the unfriendly eyes watching him. "I'm leaving."

Patrick stepped to the side, gently pushing Maggie and me back. "No one is stopping you. In fact, you've interrupted a highly enjoyable evening. Since you're too stubborn to stay and enjoy your son's talent, it's best you do leave."

My father strode by, stopping to glare at me. "Last chance, Sebastian."

I stared at him, shocked to realize I no longer had any feelings toward him. I was emotionless. "Don't want it."

"We're done."

Relief was the only thing I felt at that moment. I shrugged.

He stormed out.

I pulled Maggie into my arms. "Are you all right?"

She nodded against my chest, her arms clutching me hard. "Are you?"

"I'm fine."

I met Patrick's gaze. He clapped me on the shoulder and smiled, trying to ease the tension. He raised his voice. "What's a night out without a little drama? That's what happens when you get to be famous."

Everyone in the bar chuckled. "We prefer your singing, Sebastian!" someone shouted out.

I held up my hand. "You'll hear it in a minute. Promise."

They applauded, and I knew I was among friends who had my back. An entire roomful of them.

I looked at Finn. "Just give me a moment, and I'll start back up."

"Take your time. They all need refills now the halftime show is over." He winked and jerked his head in the direction of the hall. "My office is empty."

"Patrick?" I asked quietly.

"With you."

In the office, I cupped Maggie's face. "Are you sure you're okay?"

"I am. I was so scared he would hurt you or say more nasty things."

"His words don't hurt now, Angel. The thought of him hurting you almost did me in."

"He didn't. I'm fine."

"We don't ever have to see him again. He will never get near you again."

"Or you."

"No."

I turned to Patrick. "I will pay you back."

He grinned. "I know. Do I look at all worried?"

"As soon as I get my advance. I don't know what I owe him—"

"Whatever it is, we'll figure it all out."

"I don't get why he showed up."

"He showed up to make a point. He was so sure by now you would need him and agree to whatever he wanted." Patrick winked. "I guess you showed him."

"He won't be back, that's for sure."

"Thank goodness," Maggie muttered.

I shook my head. "Can you check Maggie out?"

"I'm fine. I didn't hit the floor. I bumped my hip."

"He touched you."

"Sebastian, I'm fine."

Just to appease me, Patrick did a quick check, making sure she was fine. Then he left us alone. I wrapped her in my arms, grateful she was with me.

"Are you okay?" she whispered.

"I am. I'm a little embarrassed by his behavior and pissed off he interrupted our night, but I'm okay."

She studied my face, worry etched in her expression. "Did you see how everyone was ready to defend you,

Sebastian? Your father was outnumbered. If anyone should be embarrassed, it's him."

"You're right. Still…"

She cupped my face, her touch grounding me the way it always did. "We can talk about it later, but really, I'm fine. I am glad he's gone, though."

"You were brilliant." I kissed her. "You stood up for me like a little lioness."

"He was a jackass."

"I know."

She lifted her chin. "I'm not sorry."

I kissed her again. "Thank you. And I'm glad he's gone too."

She smiled. "Then let's go back to our family."

I kissed again. "Yeah, Angel. Our family."

The next day, the table groaned with food. I had been smelling the enticing aromas since I woke up. It had taken me a long time to fall asleep. My father's words, his anger and indifference, had troubled me. Seeing him again unnerved me. It was Maggie pulling me to her chest, stroking her fingers through my hair and talking about the dinner, our friends, and the upcoming holidays that finally relaxed me. She was what mattered. Our life together. My father had made his choice.

I looked around the full table, smiling. Eleanor and Patrick, our pseudo parents. Connie—my grandmother—because she refused to hear the word half or step. Our friends Amber and Finn. Chris and his newfound love Mandy.

And my Maggie.

I lifted my glass. "A toast, if you will."

"Hear, hear!" Patrick said, slapping the table.

I met Maggie's eyes, leaning over and kissing her cheek.

"I followed this woman here, hoping for a new start. I never expected to find what I did. Joy. Love. Friendship. Family. Home. I found all that with all of you." I lifted my glass higher.

"But especially my beautiful fiancée. Here's to my fierce, brave, wonderful Maggie."

Everyone toasted her, and I sat down, smiling at her blush that stained her cheeks so prettily.

"Happy Thanksgiving, Angel," I murmured, leaning close.

"Are you okay?" she whispered.

I knew why she was asking. "I'm perfect."

"I love you. Thanks for being here," she added with a wink.

I kissed her softly.

"Wherever you are, Angel. That's where I'll be."

She smiled. "Home," she whispered.

And she was right.

I'd come home.

Thank you so much for reading FOLLOWING MAGGIE. If you are so inclined, reviews are always welcome by me at your retailer.

The news of a couple in Canada who met during a layover and married has been news on and off for years. While Maggie and Sebastian's story is not *their* story, it is fun to dream about what may did happen.

If you love shorter instant attraction stories with plenty of steam, my Happily Ever After Collection is four short stories that will have you falling in love with these couples.

Enjoy meeting other readers? Lots of fun, with

upcoming book talk and giveaways! Check out
Melanie Moreland's Minions on Facebook.

Join my newsletter for up-to-date news, sales, book
announcements and excerpts (no spam). Click here to
sign up Melanie Moreland's newsletter
or visit https://bit.ly/MMorelandNewsletter

Visit my website www.melaniemoreland.com

Enjoy reading! Melanie

**_Here is a sneak peek at Chapter One of The
Wish List_**

CHAPTER 1
ASHER

All around me were the sights and sounds of
Christmas. Lights were strung everywhere. Trees,
their branches so heavily decorated I was surprised
they were standing, were placed in the most
inconvenient places. Statues of Santa, reindeer, and
elves peered at me from the shelves. Gift wrap, bows,
ribbon, and tags were bright piles of glitter. A huge
display of frolicking snowmen and the North Pole was
set up in the middle of the department, and around it
snaked a lineup of children and their parents, waiting
to see Santa Claus.

They all looked miserable for different reasons.

The store was overly hot, overly bright, and overly crowded. The children wanted to see Santa—*now*—and the parents wanted to be anywhere but here. I had to agree with them.

Why the hell I did this to myself every year was a mystery.

But a few days before Christmas every year, I came to this store, walked to this department, found the one gift I required, and fled, grateful to be leaving the noise and confusion behind. Then I headed back to my quiet condo, where a good scotch and some soft classical music waited for me.

And silence.

I sat down, staring at the massive tree in the middle of the North Pole display, the fake mounds of snow and large bright-colored Christmas ornaments making my head ache. Despite my promise, I was seriously considering using my power and having the gift picked up by someone else and delivered to me. My sister, Suzy, wouldn't really know. I bought my niece's gifts that way, and she never complained. I picked the gifts; someone else had the hassle of picking them up. No complaints. Then again, Bonnie was five.

Except, I would know, and I hated lying to my sister. It was only for her that I would make this pilgrimage to this store and get her a gift she loved. One she expected each year from me.

"It wouldn't feel the same if someone else gave it to me," Suzy said once. "It's our thing."

And dammit, I loved my sister too much to let her down.

I glanced at the small bag in my hand. My job was done, and I could leave. Yet, I stayed sitting, staring at the chaos around me like a man unable to look away from a gruesome accident.

Suddenly, I heard my name being called. The voice was panicked, and for a moment, I was certain I was hearing things, until it rang out again.

"Asher!"

I rose to my feet as a woman rushed around the corner. Our eyes locked, and she hurried toward me. "Asher?"

I blinked at the stranger. Her bright-red hair glinted under the lights. It streamed down her back in a mass of waves. As she hurried closer, I stared at her creamy complexion that was covered in freckles. Thousands of them dotted the ivory skin, a large abundance of them on her cheeks and over the bridge of her nose. Her eyes were green—bright and clear like emeralds. She was small, dressed in a coat that looked too big for her, the hem almost to the floor. She carried a bag and another coat, this one smaller. And she looked upset. The need to help her hit me, and I moved toward her.

"Asher!" she called out again.

Did I know her? My name was unusual, so hearing her call it out confused me.

I stepped in front of her, halting her progress, our eyes once again meeting.

"I'm Asher. Can I help you?" I asked, laying my hand on her arm.

She blinked, her voice fraught with trepidation. She shook her head. "No. My son. I'm looking for my son. He-he disappeared."

I glanced over her shoulder, meeting the mischievous grin of a small boy I hadn't seen a moment ago. He was among the frolicking snowmen, hiding behind a mound of fake snow. I had no doubt it had to be the other Asher—her son. The red hair and freckles he obviously inherited from his mother gave him away instantly.

"Um, is he wearing a blue sweater with cars on it? And he has your freckles?"

"Yes," she gulped, gripping my arm. "Have you seen him?"

I tried not to notice how my body reacted to her touch. I could feel it—even through the layers of material separating us. I tilted my chin in the direction over her shoulder. "I think he's over there."

She spun, her entire body shuddering in gratitude as she found her son. "Asher, come here," she gasped, relief evident in her voice. "Now!"

The little boy I judged to be about five or six raced over, stopping beside his mother. "I was saying hi to the snowman, Momma."

She dropped to her knees, engulfing him in her arms. "You can't leave my side," she said, her voice thick with tears. "AJ, you scared me. I couldn't find you."

He patted her back, his small hand tapping on her coat in reassurance. He looked up at me, his eyes the same green as hers. They were sad-looking at the moment, the color dull. "I'm sorry, Momma. I could see *you,* so I thought it was okay. I won't do it again." He flung his little arms around her neck. "I'm sorry!"

She immediately began to comfort him, making soft sounds meant to soothe.

I sat back down, feeling guilty for witnessing the tender moment between them.

She stood, wiping at her cheeks. She turned to me, her beautiful green eyes watery. "Thank you."

I smiled. "Not every day I hear my name being called. Happy to have helped." I looked at her son. "Listen to your momma."

He grinned, his happy mood restored, and nodded. "I will. I'm a good boy."

Something about his grin was infectious, and I returned it. "I'm sure you are."

"Sit here while you wait for your husband," I offered, standing. The woman looked frazzled and exhausted.

"Oh no, we're good. No, ah, no husband to wait for," she rambled. "We're going to head home now."

She began to hand Asher his coat when she stumbled. Without thought, I was beside her in a second, wrapping my arm around her waist and supporting her.

"Are you all right?"

She blinked up at me, her face pale, her eyes unfocused for a moment. Then she shook her head. "Oh, I'm fine." She looked embarrassed. "It's hot in here."

"You're probably hungry, Momma. You didn't eat breakfast this morning."

A feeling passed over me as I looked down at her. A small unfurling in my chest. I held her close, liking how she felt against me. It was as if she belonged there for some odd reason. Concern hit me as her son's words sank in.

"No breakfast?" I asked. "You came into this store, this crowd, with no breakfast to sustain you?"

She shook her head, staring at me.

I tightened my arm. "Well, that won't do. Let's go."

"Go where?" she asked.

"Breakfast." I looked at her son. "You like pancakes, Asher?"

"Yes."

"Good man."

Ten minutes later, we were seated in one of the cafés in the expansive department store. I liked this one, and it was surprisingly empty, considering how busy the store was. I ordered coffee, eggs, toast, pancakes, and bacon, and chocolate milk for my little namesake. Then I turned to the pretty redhead who was still reeling in shock from her scare and my high-handedness. She regarded me cautiously.

"You know my name is Asher," I teased. "But I don't know yours."

"Rosie," she replied. "Rosie Duncan."

"Pretty name."

She lifted a lock of hair. "I came out with a full head of red hair. My dad thought it was appropriate."

"I like it."

"Your name is Asher?" her son asked. "Mine too! Did you know that, Momma?"

"Yes," she replied patiently.

He smiled. "Momma calls me AJ most of the time. So we won't get mixed up." He leaned forward, dropping his voice. "If she calls you by your whole name, look out. She is mad."

"I'll keep that in mind. Any advice?"

"Run," he said seriously.

I began to laugh, and he grinned. Rosie's lips twitched at the corner, but she still looked anxious.

I slid a full coffee cup her way after adding cream and sugar. "Drink up, Rosie."

Her brow furrowed. "How did you know how I like my coffee?"

I shook my head. "I didn't. But you need the sugar. You just had a scare."

"Momma, can I go look at the display?"

In the corner, not far from the table, was yet another Christmas wonderland. Asher seemed fascinated by it.

"Make sure your momma can see you," I admonished him gently as she nodded in permission.

"I will!"

He hurried away, standing and watching the animated scene in rapture.

"So, Asher," she said. "Do you have a last name?"

"Yes." I waited a beat.

She shook her head. "Care to share?"

I stuck out my hand. "Asher Hart. Asher William Hart, in case you need the whole name for when I'm in trouble."

She slipped her hand in mine. It was small and felt cool to my skin. The skin was pale, her fingers delicate. Her nails were short and natural, and she wore no jewelry. It was hard to release her from my grip. She blushed at my words, the pretty color suffusing her skin.

"I doubt I'll need it."

I winked. "I have it on good authority from my sister that I'm trouble."

She smiled and took a sip of her coffee. I found myself mesmerized by her actions. It was the oddest thing.

"Christmas shopping?" I asked, clearing my throat.

"Sort of. He loves coming here to Zoles," she murmured. "I did as a child too. I bring him every year."

"AJ?" I asked. "Short for…?"

"Asher Joseph."

"Ah. And how old is AJ?" I asked.

"He'll be five in January."

"You called out Asher when you were looking for him. Not AJ. Not his full name either."

"I panicked, and I wasn't thinking. It is rare I say his full name. He's a good boy."

"I can see that." I sipped my coffee. "So, you're *sort of* Christmas shopping?"

"Browsing, really. I have his gifts already." She smiled tightly. "I'm his only parent."

"His father is not in the picture?" I had assumed that somehow, but I needed to be sure.

She frowned. "No. He walked away when he found out I was pregnant. It's Asher and me."

"No family?"

She shook her head, color staining her cheeks again, this time darker. "No. They disowned me when they found out I was pregnant and not marrying the father."

I felt her hurt in the simple words and saw the flash of pain in her eyes. The high color in her cheeks was anger.

"My mother died last year. My father didn't even tell me. I heard he already remarried."

"So, you're alone."

She tilted her head, studying me. "And you?"

"I have a sister, as I mentioned. And a niece I adore. I tolerate her husband," I added with a wink. I actually liked him a great deal, and we got along well. "My business is my life, to be honest."

"Ah."

That was all she said. No inquiries about my job, my life, my financial status, nothing. She watched Asher carefully, tensing if he disappeared for a moment. I laid my hand on hers, squeezing her fingers. "He is perfectly safe in here, Rosie. I'm watching him as well."

"I was waiting to pay for his picture with Santa. I blinked, and he was gone." She shook her head. "He's never done that before. Disappeared on me. It-it was scary."

Flipping my palm, I slipped my hand under hers, unable to stop touching her. Our skin slid together, and I entwined our fingers. She stared at our hands, then lifted her eyes to mine. I wondered if she felt that odd connection I did. I hated seeing the worry in her expression. The exhaustion that showed under her eyes. Something inside me wanted, needed, to ease both negative inputs in her life. Anything that bothered her needed to be gone.

I was so shocked by my thoughts, I had to lower my head and clear my throat before I spoke.

"I'm sure it was frightening. It must be a difficult thing to be a single parent. But he's fine and safe. So try to relax."

She took in a deep breath, letting it out slowly.

"We come here every year," she said, sliding her hand away and wrapping it around her mug. I was surprised at the sensation of loss I experienced when we were no longer touching. I picked up my own mug and sipped as she kept talking. I liked the sound of her voice. Low, quiet, sweet.

"I did as a child as well," she continued. "My grandmother brought me until I was fifteen. She died then." She paused, swallowing. "Zoles always had the best Santa. They still do. And the displays are wonderful. I loved them."

"Well, obviously, AJ shares your feelings."

She smiled.

"So, you have his picture taken every year?"

She nodded, a small frown on her face. "The price skyrocketed this year. I wasn't sure I could swing it, but it's a tradition, so I scrimped and saved on some other things so we could do it. I knew AJ would be disappointed. And I couldn't bring him here to look at the displays and not see Santa," she explained. "You can't discuss finances with a small child."

I studied her. "Is that why you didn't eat breakfast this morning?" I asked.

She shook her head, looking embarrassed. "Oh, no. I was trying to get him ready, and we ran out of time."

She was a horrible liar. In my business life, I knew how to spot one, and she was one of the worst I had ever seen. But I let it go, understanding it was a point of pride for her.

But I didn't like it.

"Besides, it was on his wish list. I can't deny his wish list. He really asks for so little."

"I see." I crossed my legs. "Does his momma have a wish list?"

She laughed lightly, shaking her head. "No. Not one I would share anyway. I keep it pretty close to my chest."

I sipped my coffee, having a sinking feeling that her wish list contained far more sensible things than her son's did.

That bothered me as well, and I couldn't explain why.

Our breakfast arrived, and I filled a plate, sliding it in front of Rosie. I had ordered family style, so I knew there would be plenty. "Eat." I paused, using a word that rarely passed my lips. "Please."

AJ ran over, sliding onto a chair. He gazed at the table, his eyes wide. "Oh, Momma. This is a feast!"

I laughed and slid a pancake onto his plate and added some bacon and scrambled eggs. Rosie cut up the pancake after adding some butter and syrup to it, and AJ dug in, chatting in excitement. He pointed out his favorite parts of the display, telling me about his school, his best friend, Charlie, and his second favorite friend, Ashley.

"Sometimes she says she's my girlfriend, and I just let her," he explained. "Momma says I'm too little to have a girlfriend, but I don't like to hurt her feelings." He grinned, showing me a mouthful of pancakes. "She's nice, though, and gives me her cookies at lunch sometimes, so it's okay if she wants to hold my hand in line."

I nodded sagely, finding him highly entertaining. He had good table manners, said please and thank you, and was intelligent. Rosie was obviously a good mother.

I watched her eat, noticing her seeming love of toast. She buttered each piece liberally, adding jam and enjoying the small triangles. Color returned to her cheeks as she ate some bacon and eggs, and I filled her coffee cup again, adding cream and sugar as if I had been doing it for years. It pleased me to know I was doing something to help her—even if it was in the smallest of ways.

It struck me how comfortable I was with the two of them. None of my usual impatience or terseness was present. I laughed and teased AJ, as well as his mother. I smiled in amusement at his ramblings. Watched his momma with concern and interest.

She fascinated me. From the way she ate her toast to her quiet observations. I thought she was lovely, her red hair and freckles enchanting. On AJ, they were adorable; on Rosie, they were sexy and playful. Yet, she seemed unaware of her prettiness. Our eyes met often, locking for brief moments and speaking volumes before she would drop her gaze to her plate or refocus on AJ. I wondered if she was feeling the same draw to me as I was to her.

We finished breakfast, and I paid the bill, silencing her protests with a dark look. When we were done, she was surprised but didn't object as I took her hand and led her and AJ out of the restaurant.

"I'll drive you home." She had mentioned the bus at one point, but I didn't want to say goodbye yet. Or have them wait in the cold for public transportation.

"Oh no—" she began, but I held up my hand, silencing her.

"I'll drive you home," I repeated.

She didn't reply or make a comment as we stepped outside and my vehicle was waiting by the door. She looked nervous, and it occurred to me I was a stranger and basically demanding she let me drive her home. I called the store doorman over.

"Mr. Hart?" he asked.

"This is Rosie Duncan. I am driving her and her son home."

He tipped his hat. "Yes, sir." He smiled at Rosie. "You're in good hands, miss. Mr. Hart will look after you."

She glanced at me with a smile. "Thank you."

"I want you to feel safe."

"I do."

"Good, then let's get you home."

I was grateful I had a car seat for my niece already and I knew how to use it. When she saw it, Rosie looked startled, but I explained. "My niece and I have a standing pizza night once a month. I drive." I winked. "She's a terror behind the wheel."

Her laughter made me grin. It was light and buoyant, the sound filling the air. I liked it. I wanted to hear more of it.

I buckled AJ into the back, made sure Rosie was safe in the front, and slid into the driver's seat.

"What?" I asked as I turned to look at her, seeing the look of confusion and wonder on her face.

"Where did you come from, Asher?" she asked.

I smiled as I touched her cheek. "Your secret wish list."

Her blush said it all.

ALSO AVAILABLE FROM MORELAND BOOKS

Titles published under M. Moreland

Insta-Spark Collection

It Started with a Kiss

Christmas Sugar

An Instant Connection

An Unexpected Gift

Harvest of Love

An Unexpected Chance

Following Maggie

The Wish List

Titles published under Melanie Moreland

The Contract Series

The Contract (Contract #1)

The Baby Clause (Contract Novella)

The Amendment (Contract #3)

The Addendum (Contract #4)

Vested Interest Series

BAM - The Beginning (Prequel)

Bentley (Vested Interest #1)

Aiden (Vested Interest #2)

Maddox (Vested Interest #3)

Reid (Vested Interest #4)

Van (Vested Interest #5)

Halton (Vested Interest #6)

Sandy (Vested Interest #7)

Vested Interest/ABC Crossover

A Merry Vested Wedding

ABC Corp Series

My Saving Grace (Vested Interest: ABC Corp #1)

Finding Ronan's Heart (Vested Interest: ABC Corp #2)

Loved By Liam (Vested Interest: ABC Corp #3)

Age of Ava (Vested Interest: ABC Corp #4)

Sunshine & Sammy (Vested Interest: ABC Corp #5)

Unscripted With Mila (Vested Interest: ABC Corp #6)

Men of Hidden Justice

The Boss

Second-In-Command

The Commander

The Watcher

The Specialist

Men of the Falls

Aldo

Roman

Reynolds Restorations

Revved to the Maxx

Breaking The Speed Limit

Shifting Gears

Under The Radar

Full Throttle

Mission Cove

The Summer of Us

Standalones

Into the Storm

Beneath the Scars

Over the Fence

The Image of You

Changing Roles

Happily Ever After Collection

Heart Strings

My Favorite Kidnapper

M Moreland is a pen name for NYT/WSJ/USAT international bestselling author Melanie Moreland. She loves writing contemporary romance and needed to find a home for her *bit of naughty along with the nice.*

Insta-Spark collection from M Moreland are complete standalone reads with one thing in common - lots of sweetness and a guaranteed HEA. Instant attraction, little angst - love and happiness abounds.

Melanie lives a happy and content life in a quiet area of Ontario with her beloved husband of thirty-plus years and their rescue cat, Amber. Nothing means more to her than her friends and family, and she cherishes every moment spent with them.

While seriously addicted to coffee, and highly challenged with all things computer-related and technical, she relishes baking, cooking, and trying new recipes for people to sample. She loves to throw dinner parties, and enjoys traveling, here and abroad, but finds coming home is always the best part of any trip.

Melanie loves stories, especially paired with a good wine, and enjoys skydiving (free falling over a fleck of dust) extreme snowboarding (falling down stairs) and piloting her own helicopter (tripping over her own feet.) She's learned happily ever afters, even bumpy ones, are all in how you tell the story.

Melanie is represented by Flavia Viotti at Bookcase Literary Agency. For any questions regarding subsidiary or translation rights please contact her at flavia@bookcaseagency.com

Connect with Melanie

Like reader groups? Lots of fun and giveaways! Check it out Melanie Moreland's Minions

Join my newsletter for up-to-date news, sales, book announcements and excerpts (no spam). Click here to sign up Melanie Moreland's newsletter

or visit https://bit.ly/MMorelandNewsletter

Visit my website www.melaniemoreland.com

facebook.com/authormoreland

x.com/morelandmelanie

instagram.com/morelandmelanie

tiktok.com/@melaniemoreland